GETTING A LIFE

Sick of being the odd one out, lecturer Joanne Swithenbank books an escort to accompany her to the college Christmas formal dinner dance. But 'Rudy' turns out to be Michael Thomas, one of her mature students! Once the dinner is over, she realises she actually likes this man. Could he ever possibly fall for his tutor? Joanne dares to start believing so — until her best friend Trisha sees Michael out with another woman . . .

CHRISSIE LOVEDAY

◆

GETTING A LIFE

Complete and Unabridged

LINFORD
Leicester

First published in Great Britain in 2012

First Linford Edition
published 2015

A catalogue record for this book is available
from the British Library.

ISBN 978–1–4448–2299–1

Published by
F. A. Thorpe (Publishing)
Anstey, Leicestershire

Set by Words & Graphics Ltd.
Anstey, Leicestershire
Printed and bound in Great Britain by
T. J. International Ltd., Padstow, Cornwall

This book is printed on acid-free paper

1

There were two letters in the mail box. She picked them up. One was inevitably a bill. Weren't they always? She stared at the one with the unfamiliar writing. What *had* she done? She fingered the envelope and continued to speculate. It could only be one thing, and already she was bitterly regretting her stupid impulse. It was all Trisha's fault. How could she have allowed herself to be driven into a corner like that? She was a sensible human being. Dependable. Occasionally considered eccentric but certainly not downright stupid. Normally.

It began when a crowd of the younger lecturers from Barstow College went for drinks on someone's birthday. After a drink, it had turned into a meal and then a further session at a karaoke bar. Karaoke. How naff was that? Even worse, she had drunk enough wine to be pushed on the stage and before she knew it, she was deeply into *I Will Survive* along with Gloria Gaynor's very own backing group. The crowd went wild. She had a good voice but she never, ever, did anything like this. She'd done solos at school, but nowadays she was much more self-conscious. Just shows what a bit of encouragement and a few glasses of wine can do, she thought. They made such a fuss, she stayed on the stage and went through a brief repertoire of things from the charts, past and present. She actually began to enjoy the attention. The bar's owner came up and offered her a regular spot. Said it was good for business to have someone getting things going. Naturally she refused. She couldn't get into anything like that. She'd probably be drummed out of her job if the hierarchy ever found out. College lecturers, especially at Barstow College, simply did not do that sort of thing.

'I never knew you could sing like

that,' Trisha told her afterwards. 'You're brilliant.'

'Yeah, well, it's not the sort of thing you do in lectures.' She tried to make light of it. Even the guys were impressed and one of them, Jason something or other, took her to one side and flirted outrageously. She knew he was married and gave him the quick brush-off.

'Never knew you had it in you,' another of the crowd told her, putting his arm round her shoulders. What was it with guys? Do something a bit different and they're all over you like a rash. Want the reflected glory, she decided.

'I'm not always glued to computers,' she told them. 'I do have a life beyond keyboards.' Now if anything was a lie, that was. Doesn't do the street cred much good to admit that computers are one's entire life.

'Why don't you let me give you a lift home,' persisted Jason. 'You can't start looking for taxis at this time of night.'

'Won't your wife be expecting you?' she said coldly.

'Away. Gone to see her folks. I'm all alone for entire weekend. Footloose and fancy-free.'

'And well and truly married,' she reminded him. 'Sorry, I'm not interested.'

'Give up on her,' Trisha told him. 'She's a dedicated bachelor.'

Oh, the joys of slightly too much alcohol! Her tongue went into overdrive. Before she could regain control, she had informed the assembled company that she did in fact have a regular fellow and was practically engaged. All lies of course. The closest she had ever come to a regular boyfriend was on a package holiday with the parents ages ago. She'd spent every evening at the hotel disco with a spotty youth from Doncaster who also wanted to escape parental control. She'd even avoided most relationships at university. The others seemed so immature in her year and besides, she was determined to get

4

a First. It meant she worked like crazy and missed out on much of a social life. On reflection, maybe it was foolish to miss all that, but it had worked for her academic achievements. Her parents were over the moon with their clever daughter. A lecturing post at a young age was her reward.

'So, who's this mystery man in your life?' Trisha asked. 'When do we get to meet him?'

'I don't mix work and pleasure,' she replied haughtily.

'So, this evening is work, is it?' teased Jason.

'Course not, but you know what I mean.'

'So, are you bringing him to the Christmas bash?' Trisha persisted.

'I expect so,' she said airily. 'Haven't decided yet.' The so-called Christmas bash was still two weeks away. Plenty of time to develop bubonic plague or break some limb that would stop her from going. She loathed these affairs. Everyone was expected to dress up in posh gear and chat to the senior hierarchy before the formal dinner and dance. No such thing as karaoke there. Joanne knew there was no likelihood of being any sort of hit at that particular do.

'Right. Well, we'll arrange to meet in the pub first and get some Dutch courage. Amazing how much better the Doc's Christmas do is, after a few bevies. And we can all meet Joanne's famous bloke. Agreed?'

Everyone did agree. Especially Joanne. Idiot that she was. Where was she going to find a boyfriend in the next two weeks? If she'd managed for twenty-eight years without a single serious relationship, she was hardly going to fall madly in love in less than two weeks. And whatever could have possessed her to say they were practically engaged? There was no way out of it. She wasn't really prepared to break any limbs and nor was bubonic plague a ready option. She had eventually resorted to the small ads in the local paper and dithered over two numbers suggesting 'escorts of all types and ages'. If only she could carry it off, Joanne would save face and stop the unwelcome advances of the likes of Jason. She dialled the number and promptly put the phone down before it rang. What an idiot, she thought, as she talked herself into a second go. Press re-dial, she instructed. She held one hand down with the other to stop herself chickening out a second time.

The woman at the other end sounded quite normal and friendly. She didn't seem to find it strange that some woman of twenty-eight should be asking for an escort to accompany her to some company party.

'All part of our service,' she said. 'I'll put our contract in the post tomorrow.'

She spent the night worrying if she could phone in time to stop the woman from posting the wretched contract. The consequence of a restless night was that she woke too late to think about it, let alone actually phone. Still, she consoled herself later, she didn't have to sign the contract.

Oh, the desperation to produce the anticipated boyfriend! Trisha went on and on about it. What was she wearing? How would she do her hair? Honestly, that girl, Joanne mused. She'd never have believed she was an intelligent woman with a good job. Her mind seemed to run on pure hormones and little else. Joanne hedged about the fictitious boyfriend's name, his job, what he looked like. Trisha was furious. She even doubted his existence at one point. Joanne blushed. Then she got angry to cover it and Trisha apologised. Just as well. Her friend was quite right.

* * *

Her fingers shook as she opened the envelope. There was a nice friendly little letter with the dreaded contract. It was all very simple. The fee was payable in advance. Good business strategy, she thought. The client might duck out but at least they had the cash up-front. Her escort for the evening was to be Rudy. He was six feet tall, dark, and considered good-looking by most of their clients. Aged around twenty-five, he sounded perfect. (She had lied about her age.) He would be wearing a dark suit as requested, and the agency wished them a pleasant evening.

Pleasant? How on earth could that be? It was going to be the most humiliating evening of her life. Gritting her teeth, she wrote the cheque and posted the contract before she could change her mind.

Once over the initial panic she began to plan the actual evening. She even splashed out on a new dress. Given the choice she'd have stuck to one of her long floaty skirts. She was secretly a displaced hippy, she believed. Her parents had despaired of her long ago, wondering how they'd managed to produce an offspring who hated smart, modern fashions. In fact, their daughter seemed to be quite unlike most people of her age. Joanne was quite pleased with this image. She liked to be thought of as eccentric rather than peculiar. Much more interesting than admitting she was truly very boring.

The day of the party arrived all too quickly for her liking. It was anticipation all day at work. Trisha and the others were unbearable.

'For heaven's sake,' she burst out at lunch time. 'It's only some crummy college party, not a huge great ball. Nobody special's coming. Unless there's something you haven't told me? And yes, Trisha, I have got a real dress, not just another of my hippy skirts.'

'Great. What's it like?' she asked.

'Sort of silvery. Oh, I don't know. Wait and see.' But her friend needed chapter and verse before she was satisfied. Joanne did rather like the dress. Nothing like her usual outfits. It was close-fitting and even a bit sexy. If everything else was out of character, she may as well go the whole hog.

By five-thirty, she was sitting in her bath, liberally doused with some nice-smelling herbal stuff. She was a total nervous wreck. She felt the need of a glass of wine to accompany her to the bathroom, just to help quell the near panic.

She twisted her hair into a sort of knot with some loose ends hanging out. She wasn't entirely convinced, but loads of girls had exactly this sort of look lately. She slipped into the new dress and stood gazing at the woman who was looking back at her. The bland mop of blondish hair looked almost sophisticated. The dress clung to places she didn't expect. The neckline was quite low and even showed some cleavage. She felt even more nervous. This wasn't Joanne Swithenbank. At least, not the one she knew. She twisted round to look at the rear view. Even her bum seemed to have disappeared. Usually, she wore loose skirts, believing it hid the fact that it was far too big. She never wore trousers for the same reason. She practised in front of the mirror.

'Hi Rudy. Pleased to meet you.'

'Hi Rudy,' this time said in a sexier voice to match the dress, 'good of you to come along.' She chided herself. Idiot. She was paying the guy. She mustn't let him think there was any more to it.

The doorbell rang. Drat. He was early. She shivered violently and knew she needed the loo again. She began to wonder if needing the loo for the nineteenth time was symptom of anything contagious. Maybe she had some dreaded disease and ought to warn him off.

She found herself at the door. Opening the door. Holding it open so he could come into her totally male-free home. Once she saw him, she couldn't even speak. Tall, as described, dark, as described, handsome, as described (by most of their female clients), not called Rudy at all, as described. The familiar face stared back at her.

'It's you,' he faltered. 'You're that Joanne.'

'And you're not Rudy Whatever. What's going on? Didn't you realize it was a college do?'

'Not at all. They only told me it was a dinner and dance, following some sort of reception. At the Winterton. There was no indication that it was anything at all to do with the college. Not that I'd have known about staff events, anyhow. I'm only a humble student, after all.'

'You'd better come in then, Mr Michael Thomas.'

'You look stunning. I can't believe you didn't have a date for tonight. In fact, I'm surprised you're not safely married to Mr Right with a swarm of small Swithenbanks on the way.'

'And I find it hard to believe that you are doing something like this. Being an escort, I mean. Why are you . . . why do you?' she asked.

'Money, of course. Part-time students don't earn much and the courses are expensive. This job pays well and I enjoy it. Usually get a good meal to boot. No, I'm not in the least ashamed of it.' He smiled and relaxed. 'So, you'd better brief me on exactly who I am supposed to be.'

It felt strange, telling one of her own students all about herself. He had been in one of her classes for almost four terms now. He was taking a part-time management course as a mature student. He was a bit younger than she was. At college, it was her job to bring him up to speed on one of the computer sections of his syllabus. They didn't really know each other, apart from the course, and she'd had no idea about his part-time job.

'So, they all think we're a steady item,' she finished her explanation. 'You're my secret boy-friend. I'm sorry.'

'I'd be flattered to be your boy-friend, secret or not, but we hardly know anything about each other.'

The next half hour flashed by, as they talked about their likes and dislikes, previous friends and everything else they could think of in the limited time.

'I hope I won't let you down,' he said softly. He had a lovely voice. Gentle but positive. She could have listened to him talking all night. Perhaps she would. Well, maybe not all night.

'I think that's about all we can do for now. Let's go to it, shall we?' She sounded braver than she felt. Or she hoped she did. 'And you'll have to be Michael, not Rudy. Someone else might recognise you.'

'Pub first. Then the reception and the rest. Okay. Come along then, darling. Or maybe you have a different suggestion for what I call you?'

'Darling sounds fine. Unusual to think it refers to me, but I like it.'

She knew it was a mistake. The whole thing was a mistake. It was too late now. Somehow she had to brazen it out, like it or not. For once she had a handsome man to take her out for an evening. They could always escape from the dinner as soon as it was decent to do so. She could quite fancy spending an evening with Mike on their own somewhere. A thought struck her. She wondered if he'd be quite so happy to spend an evening with her if she wasn't paying through the nose for the privilege. She'd probably never know.

'Here we go,' she said as they arrived at the pub. They were quite late, considering there was a deadline.

'Over here,' called Jason. He was sitting next to a woman Joanne took to be his wife. She hoped her legs weren't trembling too obviously. Mike put his hand beneath her elbow and steered her towards the rest of the group. It felt nice. Warm. Comforting. To her surprise it also felt quite natural. She could get used to this. Maybe everyone else was right. She didn't know what she'd been missing.

'Hi everyone. This is Mike.'

'Haven't I seen you somewhere?' Trisha said immediately.

'Possibly. I attend the college a couple of days a week.'

'Well aren't you the surprising one,' she said to Joanne. 'And don't you look something? Why do you hide a figure like that under all those layers of skirts and scarves?'

'Don't be so personal,' her partner scolded.

'Joanne doesn't mind. Do you?' She stared at her friend again, and then allowed her eyes to partially undress Joanne's escort. Joanne could tell Trisha was impressed. She grinned. So far so good.

'What about a drink, darling,' her dreamy Mike asked. He was certainly the perfect escort.

'I'll have wine, thanks. Just a small one though. It's going to be a long night.'

'I'll bet,' Trisha said with a wink. As soon as Mike crossed to the bar, she grabbed Joanne and dragged her down beside her. 'And why have you been keeping all this so secret? Why didn't you tell me, you dope? He's simply gorgeous. I wouldn't mind a bit of that myself.'

'Hands off,' Joanne smirked.

★   ★   ★

'Just watch him like a hawk. There are several people I know who'd snatch him right away from you, given half a chance. So, how long has this been going on?'

'Oh ages,' she lied. He came back with two glasses and handed one to her. She'd given him a few quid to buy drinks etcetera. It was part of the deal and certainly better organised beforehand, rather than handing over cash in front of the others.

By the time they left the pub, she was beginning to enjoy herself. She felt relaxed, though that could have been something to do with the wine. Mike was almost too perfect. He smiled at everyone at exactly the right time. He was attentive to her at all times. She lapped it up. In fact, she thought she'd never enjoyed herself quite so much. If she didn't know herself better, she'd admit to being halfway in love with him by the end of the evening.

'You know, for a college formal, that wasn't bad,' Trisha pronounced her verdict. 'And as for you two, I shall expect to see much more of both of you. We all go for a drink sometime. And we're having a party on New Year's Eve. You're both invited. I don't accept refusals, by the way.'

Joanne gulped. Why hadn't she thought of this? Once she'd seen them together, as far as Trisha was concerned, they'd be expected to join in with every occasion going. She could never afford to pay the fees to Mike's agency very often. This was a special occasion and quite a different matter.

'I'm afraid we won't be able to accept,' Mike said, rescuing her and totally knocking the wind out of her sails. 'We always have a family party on New Year's Eve. You simply don't get out of one of my family's parties. Short of having bubonic plague, that is.'

Joanne stared at him, totally gob-smacked. He'd used the very same unlikely excuse of *bubonic plague* that she had been bandying around in her mind for the last few days. And what was this with the idea of a family party? Obviously he was simply being kind, but he sounded very convincing. She smiled and shrugged.

'You heard the man. Like he says, one doesn't get out of family parties. See you on Monday.' In a cloud of euphoria, she floated out of the room and felt that lovely, warm hand beneath her elbow. 'Mmm,' she murmured. 'I could get used to this treatment.' She hiccupped loudly, quite spoiling the moment she was hoping to create. 'Sorry,' she said as the hiccups continued.

'Hold your breath and count to ten,' he commanded. She tried but kept giggling.

'Did you see . . . hic . . . Trisha's face . . . hic . . . when you said . . . hic . . . '

'Save it till you've stopped,' Mike ordered. 'Come on. Let's get you home.'

'But I liked it . . . hic . . . ' she continued. 'In fact, it was the best evening ever, Mike. I loved it all. You're a very good man to be with. Oh, I didn't hic then. Did you notice?'

'You're crazy,' he said, laughing softly. 'I've had the best evening too. I think I should give you a refund. But I can't really because of the agency. I can give you a contribution to the drinks though.'

'Don't be silly. We had a deal. A business arrangement. But I can't afford you too often. Certainly not on New Year's Eve. Do you charge extra for a special occasion?'

'Depends. But I was serious. I'd really like you to come to our family do. It'll be ghastly, of course, but I meant it. Will you come?'

'Do you charge when you give the invite? Or do I get paid? I'll be cheaper than your rates, I promise.'

'Please Jo, let's forget all that. I'd really like to see you again.' He sounded slightly hurt, mingled with irritation.

'Joanne,' she corrected automatically. 'Don't be silly. Nobody ever wants to see me again.'

'I'll call you in the morning. Not too

early, I promise.' He leaned over and kissed her on the cheek. She touched it after he'd gone from the door . . . her door. Mike Thomas. Perhaps she would never wash that place again. She was fantasising here. Had she really drunk too much? Of course she hadn't. She was giddy with the joy of spending an evening with an attractive man, just like any normal person. What had she been missing for so long? Well, she told herself: this is the start of a whole new Joanne Swithenbank. She intended to get a life and begin to enjoy herself, before she got too much older.

She was struck by another thought. How many twenty-eight-year-old virgins could there possibly be? And how many of them would actually admit to it?

2

Joanne lay in her bed the next morning. She tried to remember every little detail of the previous evening but didn't get very far. Had she been drunk again? She didn't think so. It was a muddled memory. Had that gorgeous hunk of man really been there? Really been with her? She gazed across the room at the silver dress and knew that it must all have really happened. Mike Thomas. How on earth would she ever face him in class again? She wondered, as she began to remember the previous night in every little detail. They had spent ages talking here and had been at the college event . . . together. He had seemed quite at ease with her crowd and had even impressed Trisha and her bloke. What lay ahead? He probably had more engagements with his company. How could that work? He would be taking other women to events . . . they might even meet again at one of them. Not that that was really likely to happen as she never went anywhere.

It was Saturday. She needed to do some shopping and her place really needed a good clean-out. She needed to get up and begin to do some of her chores. The phone rang. Could this be him? Mike? She reached over and lifted the phone.

'Hallo?' she said nervously. Her voice squeaked, she realised.

'Hi. It's me.'

'Oh, Mike. How are you today?'

'I'm really very well indeed, thanks. And you?'

'I'm fine, thank you.'

'Excellent,' he replied. There was quite a long pause. 'I wondered if you'd like to go for a drink this evening?'

'Would I have to pay you?' she said without thinking.

'Of course not. Please, can't we forget about all that nonsense?'

'I suppose so. In that case, yes please.

I'd love to see you again.'

'That's great. I'll be round at seven. We could get something to eat too, if you'd like that?'

'I would. Very much. Why don't I cook us something?' she offered before she could stop herself.

'Really? I didn't know you could cook.'

'Oh, you know. Something simple.'

'I'll bring the wine then, shall I?' She thought for a moment. If he was so broke that he needed to do these escort duties, should she allow him to spend his money like that?

'No, it's all right. I'll pick some up when I go shopping.'

'If you're sure? Thanks very much. I'll be round at seven then. Bye.'

'Bye.'

Joanne put the phone down and lay back, thinking. What was she doing? Cooking for him? Buying wine for him? Like this was some sort of normal situation? He was very good-looking though. And she did really like him. She leapt out of bed, eager to get on with everything.

She drove to the nearest store and parked. She took her trolley round, picking up bits from the shelves and plonking them down. What on earth was she going to cook? What on earth was she capable of cooking? Smoked salmon. That couldn't go wrong. Starter organised. Main course? She looked in the ready meals place and picked up a chicken dish. That would do. In fact, they had a meal deal going on here. She grabbed vegetables and added them to the growing pile of things. The wine in the deal looked okay too. It may all be cheating but what else would he expect? Best of all, she'd have the rest of the day to clean up her place and make sure all was ready for his visit.

By five o'clock, the house was clean and tidy and Joanne felt exhausted. She decided on a long soak in her bath and then she would get dressed and prepare the food, such as was needed. She lay in the warm water, dreaming of the evening ahead. What would they do? Music? She wondered what sort of stuff he liked. She was bit old-fashioned in many ways and her choices were very retro. She needed to get a more up-to-date. She would download some more modern stuff before he arrived.

Suppose he wanted to go to bed? How would she cope with that one? She sat up suddenly. Her sheets. They needed changing. Oh heavens, there was so much to do. She got out of the bath and dried herself quickly. She pulled on her old things again and went into the bed-room. She grabbed fresh sheets from the cupboard and remade the bed. She wondered if she had time to wash the old ones but decided against. She stuffed them into the linen basket and hoped it would close properly. She would put it in the spare room.

Six fifteen. She needed to get the meal cooking. She looked at the instructions and transferred everything into her own dishes. The waste bin was full. She took it all out to the dustbin and emptied it. Six thirty-five. She needed to change. What should she wear? Casual? Smart? She still hadn't downloaded any music. She switched on her computer to be ready for her when she had changed.

She went into her room and decided on being casual. She took out one of her favourite hippy-style skirts and tops and put it on. She was about to do something with her hair when the doorbell rang. She ran her comb through it. It would have to do.

'Hi. You're early,' she said without thinking.

'Exactly seven o'clock,' he laughed. 'Do you want me to take a walk round the block?'

'Sorry. I didn't realise the time had gone by so quickly.'

'Are you inviting me in or shall I go for a walk?' Mike asked.

'Sorry. Come on in. Well, this is it. My home.'

'Yes, I saw it yesterday. It all looks

much cleaner and tidier,' he remarked.

'Well yes. It was Saturday today. Cleaning day.'

'I see. I'm afraid I took you at your word. I didn't bring any wine. I have brought you some flowers though.' He handed her a lovely bouquet of roses.

'Oh, how lovely. Thank you so much.' She felt suddenly shy of him. She felt her hands trembling slightly. 'Sorry, please sit down. Oh, would you like me to take your coat? Anorak?'

'Thanks. Please, relax Joanne. It's only me. Here to spend an evening with you.'

'Sorry. Yes, please sit down and relax. You look nice.' She noticed his blue denim shirt and grey pants. The shirt matched his eyes.

'You look different to last night. Well, the same as you usually look at college. Nice though.'

'Thanks. I'll just put these into some water. Oh, would you like a drink?'

'That would be great.'

'Okay. Just a minute.' She dived into

the kitchen and found a vase. How did one arrange roses? She plonked them into water and took them through. 'Aren't they gorgeous?' she said, genuinely pleased with them. 'Oh, I'll get some wine.' He was sitting there, looking . . . well, just looking. She was so unused to entertaining a man, she realised. She must shape up, she told herself. She opened the bottle of wine and returned with it and two glasses. 'Here we go,' she said, handing one to him. 'Cheers.'

'Cheers. Thank you.' They both sipped the wine. 'Nice,' he said.

'Yes.'

'How was your day?'

'Fine. Thanks for asking.' Another pause. 'And how was yours?'

'Good.'

'This is ridiculous . . . '

'This is silly . . . ' they both said at the same time. They both laughed.

'Why is this so awkward?' she asked. 'I mean to say, we spent last evening together and chatted more or less non-stop. Why is it so difficult now it's just us on our own?'

'Maybe it's the lack of other company to set us going. Why don't we talk about college? Once you get going on something you're comfortable with, it should be easy.'

Hesitantly, she began to talk about the other lecturers. It was certainly easier speaking about something you knew about. Before long, both of them were laughing and chatting as if they had never had any problems. At last, he said,

'Not being rude, but when are we going to eat? Only I didn't have any lunch and I'm starving.'

'Oh my goodness. I never put the oven on. I'll do it right away. I can bring the starter through very soon but it will be a while before the main course is ready.' She shot out into the kitchen and switched on the oven. How could she have been so stupid? She went to the fridge and took out the smoked salmon. At least he could eat that and quell the first pangs of hunger.

'Here we go. Would you like to come to the table?'

'I'd be delighted to. Lovely. I adore smoked salmon.'

'I must have known about that.' As they ate, he talked about his family. He had a brother and sister. Both older than him and both married. 'Actually, my brother is thinking of leaving his wife. All a bit nasty at present. But it won't affect the New Year's Eve party. You are still planning to come with me, aren't you?'

'I'm not really sure. I guess so. Unless anyone else turns up whom you'd prefer to take.'

'Not really likely. I've never taken anyone before. And my family don't know about my extra-curricular activities, by the way.'

'What, the escort duties?'

'Exactly that. You promise you won't tell them?'

'So, how often do you go out on such events?'

'At most, twice a week, but usually only once. It's quite well paid and I don't often have to see anyone more than once.'

'Except me. Two nights in succession. Must be getting serious,' she joked.

'I'd actually like to,' he said softly.

'What? Get serious, you mean?'

'Yes. Would that be a problem?'

'Probably. If you have to go to various functions with other women, it could get in the way.'

'Not necessarily. Still, this is only our first proper date. That was lovely. Thank you. Can I help with anything?'

'Oh no. It's all right, thanks. The rest must be properly cooked now.' She went into the kitchen and there was smoke pouring out of the oven. 'Oh no,' she cried out.

'What's wrong?' he said, coming into the kitchen.

'I don't know. Something's gone crazy. I surely didn't put the oven on too high.'

He rushed to the oven and switched

it off at the wall. He looked at the switches.

'You put the grill on, not the oven itself. It's somewhat scorched whatever that was. Sorry.'

'Oh, I am so useless in the kitchen. I usually live on pizzas. You can't go far wrong with pizza.'

'I agree. So what was that exactly?'

'Oh, I don't know. Chicken something or other. I might as well confess. It was a ready meal. The vegetables are all useless too. Oh Mike, I'm so sorry. It was a mess from start to finish.'

'The starter was good.'

'What could go wrong with smoked salmon? I ask you. What do you want to do now?'

'We could always phone for a pizza.'

'We could. Shall I?'

'Go on then.' She phoned the company she had used before, and before long the doorbell rang. They both tucked in, though Joanne gave up before she had eaten all of hers.

'Don't you want that?' Mike asked.

'No more. I'm stuffed.'

'Can I eat it then?'

'Course. I did make a pudding. No, honestly, I bought a pudding. No more pretending.'

'Good. That's what I want to hear. So, what is it?'

'Just a sort of mousse. Nothing too filling. While you finish off, I might just go and rescue the oven. Chuck out the burned mess and see what the damage is.'

She went into the kitchen, no longer smoke-filled. She threw away her special meal offer and gave a sigh. It wasn't too bad and wouldn't take much cleaning.

'Would you like some more wine?' she asked.

'Wouldn't say no.'

'Okay. I'll get some. I wasn't sure how you'd arrived here. Have you driven?'

'I came on my bike,' he confessed.

'On your bike? As in cycle?'

'Indeed. I don't have a car. Well, not an actual car of my own. My flatmate and I sort of own one between us. It was his turn to use it tonight. Mine for the rest of the week.'

'Doesn't that get difficult? With your work, I mean?'

'Not really. I usually get a taxi. It's quite easy really. Taxis are quite good around the town.'

She opened another bottle of wine and poured them a glass each.

'So, where do you actually live?' she asked.

'Flat. Across the park and in a side street. Not far at all. I can always walk back if necessary, so no worries about drinking too much.'

'That's a relief. I wasn't even sure if I should offer you more wine. I'll get the pudding now, shall I?'

'Come and sit by me,' he asked her. 'You're bouncing round like a stray tennis ball.'

'That's not very flattering,' she said, laughing as she went to sit by him.

He took her wine and set it on the small table beside him. He slipped his arm round her and drew her close to him. His kiss sent her senses reeling. She felt light-headed and sensuous and as if nothing really belonged to her any more. It must be the wine, she thought, and stayed exactly where she was to enjoy more of this man.

'Wow,' he said at last. 'I'm not sure what's happening to us but that was quite something.'

'I agree. What was in that last glass of wine? It had a weird effect on me.'

'I suspect it was nothing to do with the wine. You know, I suspect it could be us. We have both been looking for each other for a long time. Now we've found each other, everything's coming together.'

'Something's come together for me anyway. Kiss me again, please.' He obliged. It was almost an hour later when she asked if he was ready for pudding.

'I guess that would be some sort of idea. Then I think I should leave. Unless . . . ?'

'Maybe you should go. It's all a bit

quick for me to come to terms with. I like you a lot. But I need a bit of time.'

'Okay by me. I feel the same about you. I like you a lot but I'm not sure I'm ready for more just yet.'

Feeling sobered at these thoughts, they ate their pudding. It was close to midnight and getting rather cold outside.

'Will you be okay?' Joanne asked, slightly nervous there could be snow drowning him before he reached his home.

'I'll be fine,' he assured her. 'I'll see you again soon?'

'Tuesday afternoon, if my memory serves me right.'

'Tuesday afternoon. You're quite right. How on earth do you remember such events?'

'I have that sort of mind.'

'I'll work on mine. Thanks for a lovely evening. Burnt special meal and all.' He leaned over and kissed her once more. 'Just one little thing to remember me by.'

'Go home. And please, take care. I

don't want you slipping over.'

'No worries. I'll walk and push my bike. Bye.'

'Bye.' She watched as he walked away. She very nearly called after him to come back but common sense told her not to. She went back inside, shivering at the change in the weather. Still, it was early December. What else should she expect?

The next couple of days went by in a whirl. Sunday she went to see her parents. She told them she had met someone and they'd spent some time together. Her mother was thrilled and began to make plans.

'You ought to bring him over at Christmas. The whole family will be here and it would make everything just wonderful.'

'Hey Mum, not so fast. We've only been out a couple of times.' She refrained from mentioning that she had paid handsomely for the first occasion and the second was only the previous evening.

'Well, the offer's there. Think about it. And let me know soon.'

'I'll think about it. I'm sure he won't want to come though. He has a family too and they are certain to want him to go to them.'

'Well, don't let him persuade you to go with him.'

'Oh, I'm sure he won't. I'm going to them at New Year.'

'Well now, it seems only fair that he should come here with you at Christmas.'

'I'll think about it,' she promised. Was she ready for this whole family thing yet? She really didn't think so.

Back at her house that evening, she gave thought to the whole business of Christmas. Horrible affair, was Christmas. All the family jollity and everyone getting together. She would have liked a good book, a frozen dinner and time alone. But that was unlikely to happen. Should she invite the lovely Mike? She would give it some thought. Meantime, she couldn't wait to see him again on Tuesday afternoon.

3

The feeling of excitement was still with her when she awoke the next morning. She stared at herself in the mirror. Same Joanne. No changes. But inside, she knew that she had made a break-though. She had come alive. The years when she felt slightly scared of men were over and done. She'd first felt this fear of looking foolish when she'd gone out with a whole group of people at university. She had very quickly realised she was the outsider. Joanne had been to an all-girls' school and never really had much to do with the opposite sex. The main problem she seemed to have developed was when talking socially to a group. Without wishing to blow her own trumpet, she realised she probably knew more than most of them. She was very bright. She also learned that most members of the male species feel threatened by a clever woman. What a crushing bore she must have been. No great interest in pop music; preferred the more serious, arty films (apart from her addiction to rom-coms); rarely went to concerts or theatres. She honestly didn't know where her youth disappeared to. Now it was all about to change. No more Joanne. It would be Jo, from now on. She experimented with the sound of the shorter name a few times, and liked it.

After the encouraging start with Mike, she promised herself she was about to become the femme fatale of the I.T. section. If men liked the occasional helpless-little-woman act, she would surely be able to oblige. It would probably take some doing but she was certain she could manage it. She was actually planning major life and character changes. Unfortunately, she was unable to start making changes right away as she was teaching for all of the day. She felt exhausted by the time she arrived home. She heard the phone ring, then noticed the answering machine flashing and was tempted to delete the message without playing it. It was bound to be her mother but she played it anyway. She played it a second time, unable to believe what she heard.

'Hi Joanne. Just wondered if you're free this evening? I fancied a film. Call me back.' There was a number. The voice was unmistakable. Mike. He'd actually called. He'd said he would, but most people said that and never did. She pounced on the phone and dialled the number he'd given. She was shaking slightly . . . nervous tension, she supposed. His answering machine cut in.

'Sorry . . . machine speaking. Why don't you speak to it? It always tells me who called, provided you tell it who you are.' She laughed softly. Nice message.

'Hi Mike. Just got your message. Bye.'

She put the phone down and cursed

herself. If she had answered it right away she might have been in time to catch him. What would Trisha have done? Undoubtedly she would have made some move or suggestion. She tried ringing again. The phone was engaged. Odd. She dialled again. Still engaged. She put her phone down. She could try again later. Her phone rang and she pounced on it.

'Hallo dear. Only me. How are you?'

'Oh, Mum,' she said, the disappointment clearly showing in her voice.

'I'm sorry to disappoint you,' she snapped. 'I just wondered if you've asked him yet. For Christmas,' she added.

'I'm a bit busy at the moment,' she said, wishing she'd take the hint and clear the line.

'Oh, that's nice.' Jo mouthed the words with her. She went on talking for ages.

'Look, I haven't seen him again. But I will ask him. Gotta go now. Bye.'

Suppose Mike was trying to call back? He'd be going out again if she didn't call soon. Mike's number. Still the answer phone — then his voice cut in.

'Jo? Sorry, Joanne. It's Mike.'

'Not to worry. Sorry I missed you.'

'Your phone was constantly engaged for about half an hour,' he accused. 'I tried to call you right back but . . . '

'My mother.'

'I'm sorry. I'm afraid I'm working after all. A late call-up. But I'll see you tomorrow?'

'Oh, of course. You're bound to be booked up anyway, at this time of year.' She felt like weeping. She couldn't bear the thought of him being charming to some other woman. Dammit, she could have booked him herself, if she'd only thought of it.

'I'm really sorry. I have to go now. I'll see you tomorrow.'

She put the cover over the computer, just for the sheer novelty of not staring at the blank screen. She usually spent hours writing programs and trying out various experiments during the evenings.

But not this one. It was almost nine when she finally sat down with some tinned spaghetti for supper. She wondered what Mike was doing. Was he eating a sumptuous meal with a lovely lady? She hoped not. She tossed the remains of the spaghetti into the bin. It tasted like tomato-flavoured cardboard. She opened a bottle of wine and sat sipping it, wondering which colour wine he was drinking. She hated this job of his, and promised herself she would find out why he did it and if it was really necessary. Not that it was anything to do with her, of course.

It was a restless night. It was freezing cold in the bedroom. Jo always thought it was healthy to sleep in a cold room, but by three o'clock in the morning she decided it was sheer stupidity and switched on the heating. She then fell deeply asleep and didn't wake until eight-thirty.

'Help,' she squeaked. Just when she wanted to look nice for Mike at college that afternoon, she woke late and had to rush. She showered in seconds, made some coffee and still just made it to her lecture by nine-fifteen.

When Mike arrived, along with several others in her class, she felt her heart leaping again. He was still as handsome as she remembered and still as charming. She delivered her class and set them all tasks to work on. Her heart beating faster than she was used to, she stopped beside him.

'Hi,' she said softly.

'Hi yourself. You look nice.'

'Not sure why. I dressed in seconds this morning. Sorry, I mustn't chat like this to you. I'll see you afterwards?'

'Okay. Sounds good.'

When the class finally reached its end, she made her final speech.

'There is only one more week before we break for the Christmas holiday. Make sure you bring everything, won't you? I need your coursework in next week. Thanks.'

The usual buzz went on in the room, and soon she was left with Mike.

'Shall we get a drink in the café?' he asked her.

'Okay. I'll just switch off everything and I'll be with you.'

They went to the main café, now full of students.

'Is there a table anywhere?' he asked.

'I'll go and look. I think there's one in the corner.'

'I'll go for coffees if you can grab it.'

'Sorry about last night,' he said when he arrived. 'I thought I was going to be free but a late call came in.'

'I was disappointed. Why do you really do it? Be an escort, I mean?'

'Why did you book an escort?'

'Because I didn't want my friends to know I don't have a boyfriend. Not a real one, I mean.' She blushed as she spoke. It seemed such a shameful thing to have to admit.

'So, there you have it. That's why I do the job. There are lots of female escorts on the agency's books, too. So it isn't just females who don't like going to functions on their own. I need to earn some extra money and this is one way to do it. One thing I must say — I simply don't understand why you haven't got a whole swarm of men in tow.'

'Probably because I'm too fussy. And I'm quite brainy. Men don't like that. If I know more than they do, they soon get bored. Emasculated or something.'

To her surprise he laughed like mad. She felt annoyed. What had she said that was funny?

'An intelligent woman is a delight,' he said softly. 'You wouldn't believe how difficult it is to look interested when some woman drones on about clothes or make-up. Honestly, they do. They seem to think I'm actually interested in what they bought in the town or how long it took to change their hair colour.'

'I have the same problem with my female colleagues. I'm boring because I love my work, and if I talk about it outside the college, I'm booed.'

'I can understand that. Typical of the world really. It's quite tough being a

49

mature student. Most of the rest of the groups are rather young. I have to make it work though, for my family's sake.'

'Why?'

'We have a family business. Small manufacturing ... electronic components. My father runs it and my sister and I both work there. We need to develop various new projects. I'm also updating various systems and it appears that I need to have a recognised, formal qualification. Meantime, I also need to earn extra money.'

She listened to his story. He must work very long hours, trying to fit in his college stuff and everything. She had never enjoyed such closeness in such a short time.

'I'm really sorry,' she told him. 'I never should never have gone on nattering for so long. You should have stopped me.'

'Nonsense, I'm really enjoying the conversation.'

'I don't know how we're going to manage to form any sort of relationship with all you have to do,' she said.

'Won't be easy,' he smiled. 'I'll try to find time to fit it in, if you're willing.'

'You mean, you actually, want to . . . ? Great.' She sat blushing.

'Jo . . . sorry, Joanne,' he began. She remembered her decision.

'Jo will do just fine,' she said with a smile.

'Jo, then. You must stop putting yourself down so much. You're a gorgeous, sexy woman. You have a good wit and excellent conversation skills.' She finally blushed as if there were no tomorrow.

'I'm good with animals and hate small children,' she added frivolously. 'None of it comes naturally to me. You are perfectly charming to everyone.'

'There you go. You have to learn to accept compliments. I really mean what I say. The charm is purely a role I play. I'm actually quite shy, out of my actor's role.'

'I don't believe that, not one bit of it.'

'Do you fancy a film?' he asked suddenly. 'There are one or two I'd like to see, if you're in the mood.'

'Why not?' she agreed.

They went to the little town's one and only cinema. She was actually surprised to discover that there were several theatres within the building and several films were on offer. Just shows how stupid and out of touch I am, she was thinking.

'Our own little multiplex,' she murmured.

'Miniplex, more like,' he laughed.

It wasn't a bad film, but sitting so close to him she felt slightly unnerved. She kept wanting to touch him. To feel his arm round her, like the couple in front of them. She left her hand lying casually on her lap, near to his. What a kid she was. He bumped into it at one point and looked at her. He smiled and, joy of joys, he picked it up and gently pressed his lips to her fingers. She felt such a rush of whatever it was, she nearly burst with pleasure. She smiled in the darkness and squeezed his hand back. She'd never dare tell anyone about how she felt. Most twelve-year-olds today had already experienced the sort of emotions she was going through. If only she wasn't so pathetic. She had honestly never felt such pleasure in touching another human being. Of course she had touched other people . . . kissed friends and colleagues, but never had this sort of reaction. Did love at first sight have a grain of truth? But even if it did, she'd certainly seen Mike for several months at college. He was one of her students, after all. Had she felt attracted to him at any other time? She couldn't remember anything. But her mind was always focussed at college. And there was the small matter of a dozen or more other students in the room.

She could hardly wait for the film to end.

'Shall we have a drink and something to eat?' Mike asked as they left the cinema. His hand was tucked under her arm. Just as it had been on Friday at the dance.

'I don't really think I want one. We could have coffee back at my place.'

'Sounds good. I mustn't be too long though. Early start tomorrow.'

'Know the feeling,' she sympathised. 'We've only got a week more to go before the Christmas break.'

'About the New Year's Eve party. I really meant it when I asked you to come with me.'

'Thanks. I'd like that,' she replied, a warm glow sweeping over her. Something to look forward to: a family party. It could never be like one of her family's parties. No Aunty Ethel singing her heart out about some ancient old crone called Sally, living in an alley.

'It will be quite a large party in the village hall near my grandparents' place. It's a reunion to celebrate the Australian contingent's visit. Can't think why they want to come to the UK in the middle of winter.'

'What should I wear?' she asked in sudden horror. She didn't fancy going through the pain of buying another dress she'd only wear once.

'Would you wear that glorious silvery thing again? I loved it. You'll have the entire male membership of the family ogling you. But I'd actually rather like that.'

'OK. If it you think it's suitable.' She smirked inwardly. It all sounded very promising.

They swapped notes on their respective prospects for Christmas itself. She told him how duty-bound she felt, being at home and suffering from terminal boredom. Same old jokes about the turkey, same old routine with crackers, unfunny mottoes and paper hats.

'Sounds quite peaceful compared with my lot. I get nearly demented with my brother's and sister's kids. They seem to go to bed at midnight and be up again by about three. I did think of bailing out and going away somewhere. But that's not much fun on your own.' Mike looked thoughtful.

The idea hit her at almost the same

moment as the words were streaming out in full flow.

'You could always come home with me and help save my life,' she blurted out.

'Er . . . ' he mumbled, looking shocked. Bad idea, she thought.

'Sorry. I shouldn't have said that. It came out before I thought. Of course you wouldn't want to spend a totally boring time with my parents. In any case, my mother would expect us to announce our wedding day before the roast potatoes were dished out.'

'Can I think about it?' he asked. 'If it was a serious invitation, I mean?'

'I was half joking,' she responded, her jaw still somewhere down on her chest. 'You don't have to think about it. I wasn't really serious,' she added lamely. Poor bloke was obviously totally embarrassed. She'd put him in a real spot now.

'I . . . well, I'd like to come with you. Trouble is, I'm working on Christmas Eve and won't be free to leave until Christmas morning. I can't actually work out how I could escape the family net at our place that late in the festivities.'

'Please don't worry. I was only . . . well . . . thinking how nice it would be to have something to look forward to. It wasn't a good idea. Forget I said anything.'

Back at home, she made two mugs of coffee and started to chat about any irrelevancies she could think of. She felt acutely embarrassed and just wanted him to go. Why did she seem to spend half her life wanting something to happen; and when it did, she couldn't wait for it to be over?

As she showed him to the door he caught her hand. He pulled her towards him and wrapped his arms round her. She waited with her eyes closed for the kiss that she knew was coming. So incredibly gently, his lips touched hers. She waited for the world to begin turning again and held her breath. The gentleness gave way to a firmer, more insistent pressure and she responded. At this moment in her life, she knew she'd fallen in love. She could feel his warm breath on her cheek. She could feel his heart beating against her body. She could sense his blood as it coursed through his veins. She wanted it to go on for ever. She clung to him as if trying to pull his very essence to her. She released his lips briefly, intending to take a much needed breath. He gasped and pulled her back. Obviously, he was feeling something of the same intensity as she was. She lost track of time as they stood, cramped in her tiny hallway. When he stopped for breath a second time, he murmured in her ear.

'I think I should stop kissing you now, or I will never be able to stop.'

'Fine by me,' she said, pulling him back. His body scent filled her nostrils, bringing with it a whole new flood of desire.

'Jo, darling Jo, I have to leave. This is too fast for both of us. Don't let's spoil anything. Not just yet.'

'I'm sorry.'

'Hey, don't look like that,' he

laughed. 'All I'm saying is, let's savour what is growing between us. Don't let's rush things and use up what could be very precious times ahead; special times. We can make a long voyage of discovery and who knows where we shall end up? I must go now. It's late.'

After he'd left, she leaned against the door feeling like a lovesick adolescent. At last she really did have someone special in her life. If Trisha plagued her with questions, there was something to talk about. Really something.

The final days of term passed in such a whirl of activity that she hardly had time to think. When they finished, she realised she hadn't heard anything at all from Mike. He hadn't even been to college that final day. She hoped nothing had gone wrong, or worse still, that she hadn't been dreaming at the weekend. After the inevitable last evening of drinks at the pub, the gang were swapping details of the joys of the coming Christmas. It seemed that every single member of the group was dreading the prospect. It occurred to her that if everyone hates it as much as they say, why does everyone make such an effort? They all claimed to love their families, yet dreaded spending time with them over Christmas. Maybe it was the inevitability of everything that dampened the spirits. Her father, of course, was the exception. Which colour slippers she'd bought this year was his only surprise. She wondered if they were to be in for a huge surprise this year. On the other hand, she'd heard nothing at all from Mike. It had been one of her very worst ideas ever.

'So,' Trisha was saying. 'Is he coming home with you?'

'Who?'

'Who do you think? The gorgeous Mike, of course.'

'I'm not sure. He has things to sort out and a large family to organise.' Joanne was blushing hard, she knew it. Obviously, Trisha had successfully read her thoughts during the temporary detachment of her body from her brain.

She stared at Joanne curiously. To her great relief, Trisha let the subject drop and concentrated on another bottle of wine.

After a curry and calls of 'have a good one', Joanne finally arrived home just after ten. She glanced at the machine and the light was flashing to indicate a message. Her knees went weak as she sensed it would be Mike calling. He said it was seven o'clock as he called and was she free for the evening? Typical. The next message was left at nine and a third at ten. She must just have missed that one. Unfortunately, he left no real message, so she was left wondering. She dialled his number. The sound of his voice set her heart pounding.

'Hi. Sorry to miss you earlier.' She hoped she didn't sound too anxious.

'Is your invitation for Christmas still on?' he asked.

'Well . . . ' She hesitated, heart pounding madly. 'Yes, if you want it to be.'

'I think I've managed to wangle the

evening off, after all. Christmas Eve, I mean. If it works out, we can travel to your family that evening, but I'm afraid I'd have to leave Boxing Day. How does that sound?'

She swallowed, hoping to drown the lump that had appeared in her throat.

'Sounds great,' she squeaked. 'I just hope you don't regret it. My family can be quite tedious.'

'You'll be there. That's what matters most. I really want to spend time with you. Besides, you'll be doing me a favour. I was dreading the prospect of the family fun day they all plan at my place.'

'Maybe,' she said. 'I'll call Mum right away. She'll be over the moon, I'm sure. Just hope you can cope with her constant questions. You do realise you'll get the third degree from her? And she's no idea what the word subtle means.'

'I'll practice between now and then,' he said with a laugh. 'One more favour. Will you come shopping with me on Saturday? I'll need your help to choose presents for them. You might help with some of my family's too. I'm working for the evening, but we can spend the day together.'

They chatted for a while and finally ended so she could convey the news to my mother.

'Why are you ringing so late dear? Is everything all right? You're not changing your mind about Christmas I hope?'

'Mum. Please stop and listen. I'm sorry it's late but I've been out.'

'I've just made our cocoa. Get on with it or it will be cold. I said to your father, should I . . . '

'Mum. Please.' If she hadn't interrupted, they'd have reached Christmas Eve before she got the message. 'Of course I'm coming. But it will be a bit later than usual.'

'Oh dear. Your father will be disappointed. You know how he likes his little rituals.'

'There is a bit of compensation. I'd like to bring a friend.' Silence followed.

After a moment or two, she could hear a muffled conversation going on. Obviously, the message was being relayed to her father.

'Are you still there?' Mum asked.

'Of course.'

'So who is it? This friend?'

'His name's Mike. He's, well, he's in one of my groups. And we've been seeing each other.'

'A student?' she said in the same tone Lady Bracknell asked about handbags.

'He's a mature. Almost the same age as me,' she lied.

'I see. What's he like? And why haven't you mentioned him before?'

Wearily, she tried to give the requisite information in summary form and failed miserably.

Saturday was great fun, if somewhat crowded. Along with all the other last-minute shoppers, they fought their way round, trying to decide what to get for the various family members.

'I'll pick you up about four on Christmas Eve, if that's OK?' Mike suggested as they were parting. 'I can't get away any earlier than that.'

'Fine. Mrs Whatsit from number six will have to manage without me for once.'

He kissed her, not like that first time, but much more like two old friends parting. She felt disappointed, but accepted his need to work. She found it sickening to think of him with someone else, albeit a client, just as she had been.

It was a long, dreary evening. She wrapped the presents and wrote cards for them. She was mooching in front of the television when the advert came on.

'What have you bought for your man this Christmas?' the sexy woman was saying suggestively.

'Certainly not what you're suggesting,' she told the screen. She froze. She hadn't bought him anything. What on earth could she buy for him? She realised just how little she knew about him. She didn't know what music he liked. What clothes he liked or his size. Had he got a watch? She thought of calling Trisha to ask for her advice. Then, out of the blue, her friend rang. To Joanne's surprise, Trisha asked if she could come over for coffee. A unique request, in their history. When she arrived she was ill at ease and Jo knew she had something to say. She sat Trisha down with coffee, and eventually asked straight out what the matter was. She assumed she'd had a row with her bloke. They were always rowing.

'I don't know how to break this to you. Not without hurting your feelings.' Trisha could be very nice at times but she was distinctly nosy.

'Go on,' Joanne prompted.

'It's about Mike. Just how serious are you two?'

'What do you mean?'

'Well, I saw him last night. We had dinner at that new place down the main road. I'm sorry love, but he was there. With someone. It was a party of four but he was definitely with one of the women. A rather good-looking redhead, actually. He seemed very attentive and, well, just as attentive as he was to you at the college dinner thing.'

Joanne sat nonplussed. She simply didn't know what to say, not without admitting the truth about how they'd met. Her friend took it that she was dreadfully upset to discover she was being two-timed. It wasn't like that, of course.

'There's more. He was using a false name. They were calling him Rudy. I thought that was distinctly odd. At the end, we were all leaving around the same time. I saw him driving her in a huge great car; really expensive-looking. I'm so sorry Joanne. But I thought you should know before you got into anything . . . well . . . too deep.' She didn't know whether to laugh or cry. This was all she needed. Her own doubts had largely been dispelled. She had accepted the situation with some degree of equanimity, even though she hated it.

'I'm seeing him tomorrow,' she finally managed to say. 'We'll talk it through then.'

'If you need a shoulder to cry on, you

know where I am,' Trisha offered.

'I'll be fine,' she said without much emotion. 'Don't worry. And thanks very much for your concern.'

After she'd gone, Joanne sat thinking. Trisha would say she was weak if she continued to see Mike, but she had every intention of doing so. After all, she knew exactly why he was out with his other client, didn't she?

4

It was difficult to sleep that night. Joanne kept thinking of him . . . Mike . . . being out with someone else. Though she knew exactly what his escort job entailed, it wasn't so easy knowing he was seeing someone else, making them feel as special as he'd made her feel at the college formal. This was what it was all about, wasn't it? She didn't like it much but she had to put up with it. The next day was Christmas Eve and she only had a brief time in the morning to go shopping.

She went to the shops and wandered round seeking inspiration. She looked at clothes . . . definitely not, she thought. She looked at music but there was nothing that struck her. She really didn't know this man well enough to know what to buy for him. In desperation, she finally bought him an arty book with wonderful photographs in it. She hoped to goodness he'd like it and see it as a suitable present. She wondered what he'd got for her and whether he'd had similar problems.

She got back at lunchtime and ate a quick sandwich. She felt nervous about the coming events and as she dressed, she wondered about the sleeping arrangements at her parent's house. It might be tricky, but somehow she didn't feel as if it was going to matter too much. Did she want to sleep with him? Of course she did, but wasn't sure how it would be. Would he be shocked that she was a virgin? Would he hold it against her? She heard someone knock at her door and shot down the stairs so quickly she almost fell.

'Oh, it's you,' she said as she opened the door. 'I wasn't expecting you just yet.'

'I got away a bit earlier than I planned. I thought I'd come round anyway to see if you were ready.'

'Lovely to see you. Come in. I take it you won the car this weekend? Well, I know it isn't really the weekend, but you know what I mean.'

'Indeed I did win the car battle. Mel wasn't too thrilled but hey, it's Christmas. Come here you,' he said, pulling her close to him. He kissed her very thoroughly and when she was feeling weak and past caring, suggested they had some coffee. She blinked at him, surprised at the suggestion. 'I'm sorry, I didn't quite know how to stop kissing you,' he announced.

'I see. I wasn't quite sure myself,' she mumbled and went into the kitchen and put the kettle on. 'I've actually got quite a lot of stuff to take: plenty of presents and a whole lot of clothes, etcetera. I hope there's going to be enough room for them.'

'I'm sure there will be. My things aren't too voluminous. I'm looking forward to meeting your family.'

'I hope you won't be too disappointed. I'm not quite sure how they'll react to you,' she said, as she made the coffee. They sat at the kitchen table to drink it and catch up on what had been happening since they'd last met.

'I hope you're not scared off by them. They do tend to be a bit noisy.'

They drank coffee and she told him all about the members he was about to meet.

'Dad likes to do the parade along the street on Christmas Eve. I told you that. He may be a little merry by the time we get to them. He drinks sherry or wine at each place he stops. I usually go with them but it's been nice not to go for once. I hoped once I got out of going, everything would be plain sailing after that.'

They finished the coffee and Joanne went upstairs to fetch her bag. He was standing looking out of the window when she came down. He smiled at her and then hesitated.

'Look, I don't know what you've said about me. I assume you haven't told them how we met?'

'Of course not. I said you were one of my students. I said you were one of the matures, by the way.'

'Oh dear. Does that mean I have to be serious or something?'

'Not at all.'

He paused again.

'I wanted to know . . . I meant to ask you if you knew what the sleeping arrangements would be? I mean, I'd be delighted to sleep with you, but as it would be the first time . . . '

'Don't worry about it. I can't believe my mother would ever allow me to sleep with anyone until we were married.' He looked greatly relieved.

'I just wanted it to be very special when we do. I should probably say *if* we do.' She felt the colour rising on her cheeks and she looked away.

'Shall we load my stuff into your car?' she asked. Anything to change the subject. She didn't want to spoil the next couple of days.

They set off to drive the short distance to her old home. It felt strange to be going with someone else in a different car.

'Who were you out with the other night?' she asked.

'I don't know. When do you mean?'

'A glamorous redhead, she was described to me.'

'Oh, that was some woman who wanted a partner for the evening. I went as I was free. Why do you ask?'

'Trisha saw you and, being as she is my best friend, felt duty-bound to come and tell me you were two-timing me.'

'But I wasn't. I was going to tell you anyway. She really was a crushing bore: all bright and sparkly, and wanting to be seen to be accompanied by this dashingly handsome young man.'

'I see. And how often have you been out with her?'

'Three or four times now. She likes me to drive her car too.'

'And calls you Rudy?'

'And she calls me Rudy. You really mustn't be jealous you know.'

'I'm not. Well, not really. Okay, I am pretty jealous.'

'Well you've no need to be. She's a

client. She did once invite me to a party but I refused her.'

'You mean she wasn't going to pay you?'

'Something like that.'

'Turn left down here,' she said realising they were almost there. 'It's the third place on the right. No, not this one, the next.'

'Wow. Pretty posh down here isn't it?'

'I s'pose so. It's just home. Has been all my life really. You ready for all of this?'

'I'm ready,' he told her. He leaned over to kiss her and she gripped his hand.

'Let's go then. We'll come back to unload the car later.'

They went to the front door and pushed it open.

'Hi,' she called out. 'Anyone here?'

'Joanne and Mike. Welcome. Come on in.' Joanne's mother was an older version of her daughter and seemed quite relaxed. 'Did you have a good drive?'

'Not at all bad, thank you,' Mike said as he shook hands with his hostess.

'Who's here?' Joanne asked.

'Only the two of us. Dad's having a snooze to get over his lunchtime excesses and your brother and family are due any time now. I'll show you up to your rooms if you want to unpack your stuff from the car.' They went out again to collect everything and took it all up the stairs. 'I've put you in separate rooms, but if you want to . . . '

'That's fine Mum, thanks. Am I in my old room?'

'Well, I thought perhaps you'd like to give that to Mike and you can go in the box room. I've had a clear-out.'

'That's fine. Thanks.'

'Hey, don't let me put you out of your room,' Mike said forcibly. 'I'll be fine in the box room.'

'I'll leave the pair of you to decide. I'll go and put the kettle on. Come down when you're ready.'

'We will. Thanks Mum.'

'So, this is your old room? I like it.

Girly, but not too bad really. Not the worst I've seen,' he teased.

'How many others have you seen?'

'Not a lot. Where's the box room then?'

'Next door to this one. It's really quite small. Are you really sure you don't mind it?'

'Quite sure, thanks. Now, can we stop being formal and get on with Christmas?'

They went down and the rest of the family turned up. She hadn't seen her brother Geoff for ages and they were soon wrapped in conversation. Mike seemed to have linked up with Geoff's wife and they were chatting nineteen to the dozen. The two kids had gone to find her father and wake him up.

'Auntie Ethel will be here tomorrow morning, I'm afraid. Dad has to go and fetch her and a friend from the nursing home. There will some other people dropping in during the morning. You know your father. He invited them round after today's little outing. Hope you won't mind if we have a slightly late Christmas dinner?'

'Of course not,' Joanne told her. 'Whatever you plan will be fine for us, won't it, darling?' Why had she said that? She never called him *darling*. She never had called anyone darling, except at the college Christmas do. Okay, darling was an alright word. He smiled at her and she felt her heart sing. He wouldn't care what she called him, she realised.

'Absolutely, just fit us in with whatever you've planned. We're quite amenable, aren't we?'

It turned into a very pleasant evening. Mike got on well with her parents and brother's family. They ate dinner and chatted very freely once the children were safely put to bed. Two very excited children were sharing a room and it took some time to get them settled.

When they all decided to go to bed, Mike and Joanne sat downstairs for a while longer. They didn't want to be parted but neither did they want to sleep together. They sat on the sofa together, cosy in front of the dying fire.

'I know we said we wouldn't, but . . . '

'It must be special,' she told him. 'Let's wait till we're back at my place.' He agreed and kissed her until she felt her senses reeling. 'But if you don't stop kissing me . . . ' He did as she asked and, hand in hand, they went up together. He left her standing outside his room.

It was four o'clock the next morning and there were shrieks of disappointment from the children's room. Joanne heard her sister in law going to tell them off.

'Father Christmas certainly won't come to two naughty children. Go to sleep and we'll tell you when it's time to wake up.'

Joanne smiled to herself. What if they had kids? She lay back in her bed, wondering what it would be like to have kids of you own. She touched the wall next to her and wondered if Mike was awake. For a mad moment she almost got up and went to see him, but managed to gain enough self-control to stop herself. That wasn't how it was meant to be. Not in her parents' house. She dozed a while longer and eventually decided to rise at six-thirty. She went to the kitchen and made some coffee and took it back upstairs. She knocked gently on Mike's door and went in. He was fast asleep and looked slightly tousled. He looked so lovely lying there; she wanted to kiss him again immediately. She put the coffee down beside him and went to the door.

'Where do you think you're going?' he murmured.

'Back down to the kitchen to drink my coffee?'

'Come here,' he said, patting his bed. 'What's wrong with drinking it here?'

'Nothing at all. Depends on how you feel about it.'

'Very happy to have you close to me.' He reached over to her to pull her close enough to kiss.

'Watch it, you nearly got a coffee bath.'

She put it down on the tiny table and leaned over to kiss him.

'You could climb in beside me,' he invited.

'I'm tempted. But the family are all around. I think I'd better sit here and . . . well, drink coffee?'

'Okay. If that's what you're comfortable with.' She sat on the bed beside him and drank her coffee. They chatted about the other people in the house and those who were coming along later. She remembered something she'd wanted to ask him.

'You said you had to be back Boxing Day. Why?'

'I have an engagement Boxing Day evening. Sorry. It's one I couldn't shed. It has been booked for ages.'

'I see. A party or something?'

'Indeed. A party. I'm to accompany an older lady. She's in her thirties and wants someone to take her.'

'Someone in her thirties? Isn't that a

bit old for you?'

'I'm not too fussy. I've escorted her before. She's quite a character actually. But don't waste time taking about her. Let's talk about today. Merry Christmas by the way.'

'Merry Christmas to you too. When do you want your present? With the family or privately?'

'How about now? I'm far too nosy to wait too long. I've got yours here too.'

She went to her room and took out his book from her stash of presents. She was going back with it when the children came rushing out.

'Auntie Joanne. What have you got there? Is it for me?'

'Aren't you supposed to be staying in your room till someone comes to collect you?'

'You won't tell anyone, will you? We're going down to see if Father Christmas has been. He might have left something downstairs for us.' The pair scampered down the stairs and she gave a shrug before going back to her man.

'What was that?' he asked.

'Just the kids being kids. Here you are. I really hope you like it.' She watched as he tore off the paper.

'Oh wow. This is terrific. Thank you so much. I love Jeremy Fortescue's work, don't you?'

'Well, yes I do actually. I'm glad you like it too.'

'I haven't got you anything nearly as dramatic. But here it is, with my love.' He handed her a small packet, carefully wrapped. She undid it carefully and opened the little jewellery box. It was a very pretty pendant.

'Oh it's lovely. Thank you so much,' she said and leaned over to kiss him. He pulled her closer and kissed her very thoroughly. She felt herself falling in love with this man all over again and immediately pulled away from him. 'We should get up,' she told him.

'As you like. I was actually rather enjoying that.'

'I was too. But there are people starting to move around. I don't want anyone to think . . . well, to think we're any more than fairly casual at the moment.'

'Is that what you think? We're just something casual?'

'No, of course not. But . . . '

'No buts. Is it because I'm younger than you?'

'No, of course not. But I'm afraid.'

'What on earth are you afraid of?'

'Nothing. It's just me. Don't worry about it all. I'm going to have a shower and then get dressed. I'll see you downstairs in a while.' She left him lying in bed and wished she had the courage to do what everyone else in her group seemed to be doing.

5

By the time they were both downstairs there were shrieks of delight coming from the lounge. The children had not been forgotten and were busily opening their stockings with their parents beside them, supervising.

'What's the plan for today?' Mike asked her mother.

'We're doing drinks at eleven and then dinner will be later. About four I think. Is that okay with you?'

'Of course. I'm a guest here. I wondered if Joanne and I might go for a walk? I'd like to see the area a bit.'

'That will be fine. It would be nice if you were here for the neighbours coming in. Well, not just neighbours, but you know what I mean. You'll have time for a decent walk before all this happens.'

'Don't you want some help to get

things ready Mum?'

'No. You go out. I'm more than happy to do it myself. Most of it is ready to bring out anyway. You go and enjoy yourselves. Get some peace away from the crowd. The woods are looking quite special at this time of year.'

'Well thank you. But I'm sure you need potatoes cooking and various stuff to be peeled or something?'

'Not at all. Go off and get some air. We'll do presents after we've eaten.'

The two of them went outside and set off for a longish walk. It was crisp and clear, perfect weather for Christmas.

'I hope all this is all right for you?' she said as they marched along through the woods.

'It's all lovely. Stop worrying about what I think. Your family are lovely. A bit like you are really.' She smiled back at him and he reached out to take her hand. It felt wonderful to be walking along with him like this. The stuff of dreams, she was thinking. A handsome man alone with her in the middle of a pretty woodland. She squeezed his hand and stopped. She pulled him towards her and kissed him.

'That was to show you how pleased I am.'

'And this one's to say how pleased I am that you are pleased.' He kissed her again.

'Come on. We'd better go back now. I hope you feel better for some fresh air.'

'I'm feeling absolutely wonderful. Thank you so much for inviting me to be with you all. It was very generous of you.'

'Not at all. It's just so good you could be here. What will your folks be doing?'

'The usual stuff. They usually go out for dinner on Christmas Day. A local hotel. I can't tell you how much I'm missing all that,' he said with heavy sarcasm. 'My sister will be there of course, and her family. They meet a whole load of other people at the hotel so they'll hardly miss me at all.'

'I'm sure they will.'

'Not really. Mum was delighted I was

coming to stay here. Which also reminds me: when you come to us at New Year, I have a favour to ask you.'

'Oh yes?'

'I wonder if . . . Well, I'd like to introduce you as my fiancée? Would you be willing?'

'Your fiancée? Why?'

'It's complicated. My parents want me to move back home to their place. I like being in my flat. I have no desire to move back to them. I just want to prove how settled I am. If you are introduced as my fiancée, it all adds to my need to stay just the way I am.'

'I'm not really sure. I hate pretence and this seems to be like lying to them.'

'Think about it anyway. We still have a few days between now and New Year's Eve. Who can tell what might be happening by then?'

'We're not likely to get engaged properly by then are we?'

'Well no. I do have a ring I can give you.'

'For keeps?' she asked sharply.

'Not just now. But who can tell what may happen in the future?'

Silenced, they walked back to the house. She felt concerned about all of this and wanted to forget it.

'I will think about it,' she promised. 'But for now, let's accomplish today's events.'

When they arrived back at the house there were several new additions to the company. The neighbours had arrived and several others. Auntie Ethel and a friend from the nursing home had been collected and the party was getting into full swing. Mike eased into the company very much more easily than Joanne; and, considering she already knew most of the people, it seemed strange to her. She picked up a couple of bottles and went round everyone to fill them up.

'Joanne. What are you doing with yourself now?' asked one of the neighbours' sons.

'Still lecturing. At the college in Barstow. I'm loving doing it.'

'Really? I never thought you'd last this long there.'

'Oh you know how it is. Nice students and interesting courses. Must press on now. See you later.' She escaped from him and reached Mike and the group he was chatting to.

'Jo, our rescuer. We've almost run out of drinks here.' He smiled at her and she felt immediately at ease.

'Can I top you up?' she asked and the party went on.

It was almost one-thirty by the time people were beginning to leave. Mrs Swithenbank had already started the turkey cooking and the children had eaten far too many cocktail snacks. They were complaining about feeling sick and their mother took them away with her for a rest. The day went on, as does Christmas Day everywhere. Mike was acclaimed as a most successful visitor. The presents they had brought had all been well received and they had also been given lovely things themselves. He thanked them all for their kindness in having him with them for the day. He was charming to everyone and even managed to persuade Auntie Ethel not to sing her usual solo. He was quite an accomplished pianist, it turned out, and he played a lot of songs that everyone could join in together. Once the children had gone to bed and the elderly ladies returned to their home, it was peaceful in the house. The remaining people sat with drinks, all feeling exhausted.

'So, how long have you two been together?' asked Geoff.

'Not for very long. It just seemed right to ask him to come over. I'm going to meet his parents at New Year.' She smiled at Mike and he smiled back.

'Well, I can see something's going on. Good luck to you both. Can we look forward to something more significant soon?' asked Joanne's sister-in-law.

'You'll just have to wait and see,' laughed Mike. 'Maybe, maybe not.'

'Now is that mysterious or what?' she replied.

'Wait and see,' laughed Joanne. 'I'm utterly shattered. Does anyone mind if I go up now?'

'Me too,' Mike added. 'Thank you very much for a wonderful day, Mrs Swithenbank. One of my very best Christmases ever.'

'Call me Ann. It's been a pleasure to have you here.'

The pair left the others and went upstairs towards their beds.

'I suspect they think we'll be sharing a bed,' she told him. 'I'm really sorry but it just doesn't seem right.'

'I respect that. But please, allow me to come and say goodnight properly.' He followed her into her room and they sat down on the bed, side by side. 'I'm not going to press you into something you don't want to do and I'm not sure I want to either. Not here at least. But we can be comfortable together, to say goodnight.' He pushed her down against her pillow and kissed her once more. He moved his hands over her until she was almost ready to give in to

92

him. She wanted him in ways she had never wanted anyone ever before. He eased away from her, telling her how much he felt for her.

'I've never wanted anyone more than I want you now. Dearest Jo, I have a feeling that it isn't going to be too much longer until . . .'

'Don't say it, Mike. I don't want you to spoil anything.'

'Have you thought any more about being my fiancée next week?'

'Not really. I will think about it. Now though, you need to go to your own room.'

'Okay. Sleep well, my love.'

'And you. Night.' They kissed again and he slipped out quietly. She lay back wondering what was going to happen. But next weekend? What was all that about? Why did he really want her to pretend to be his fiancée?

The next day, the pair left after an early lunch of leftovers. The rest were staying on till the following day and then Christmas would be over and done with for another year. Joanne's parents waved them off, and made nice comments to each other as his car left their premises.

'It's amazing how long it takes to get everything ready for these two days,' Joanne commented. 'Then it's over in no time at all.'

'I've never been able to understand why everyone gets so worked up about Christmas. I mean to say, a morning spent shopping and a bit of time cooking, it's a doddle.'

'Shows how little you know about cooking. Or getting everything ready for a family event. My Mum's been working on all of this for weeks. Shopping and ordering stuff.'

'They seemed to like their presents though. It was an inspiration to give your father that book.'

'Yes, but he was clearly disappointed not to get new slippers this year.'

'Just how long have you been buying him slippers?'

'I don't know. Ten years? Maybe more?'

'Then he'd be delighted not to have to wear them in.' She laughed. They chatted all the way back to her home. He stopped outside and went in with her. 'It's been totally wonderful. I loved your family and I will never regret accompanying you. I hope you enjoyed it too.'

'You know I did. It was lovely to have you there with me.'

'And I'll see you again very soon. What are you doing this evening?'

'I don't know. Probably watching television. There's usually something decent on.'

'Don't be too lonely.'

'I won't. And I hope you hate this evening. I hope it's a terrible party and you are really bored.'

'Oh Jo, don't say that. It's just a job, you know. I do it for some extra money.'

'Oh, take no notice of me. I'm just grumpy after a lovely couple of days with you. Go and enjoy yourself, but don't forget about me.'

'Of course I won't. Come and kiss

me goodbye. I promise I'll see you again very soon.'

'You'd better remember that. Where's the party at New Year?'

'We thought we'd use our workshop; the village hall was too expensive. Maybe you'd like to come over to help us get it ready? We're going to decorate the place up a bit and make it look like a party venue.'

'I'd love to come. Thanks. Let me know where and when and I'll be there. And okay, I'll pretend to be your fiancée. I might hold you to it, mind you.' He flickered his disapproval very briefly and she wondered why. 'Sorry. I was joking, you realise,' she told him quickly.

'I know. Sorry.' He reached for her and once more, kissed her. 'I'm getting hooked on you. I hate to leave you like this but needs must. Thank you again for a lovely Christmas.'

She watched him drive away and went back inside. It seemed very quiet in her house as she unpacked her bag and the various presents she'd been given. She made a pot of tea and switched on the television. She thought about the previous day and especially about the scene in her room. She had so nearly given way to him. It would have been most embarrassing to do so at her parents' home like that.

'Oh Mike,' she said softly. 'I think I'm falling in love with you.'

The next day or two, she decided it was time to do some college work ready for the following term. She was living in a mess, with papers strewn around the place and everything organised over the floor. There were heaps of pages she had printed, heaps of pages she had discarded and piles of books in other places. She was happily engrossed when someone knocked at the door. She glanced at her watch. It was already six-thirty. Who could this be calling on her? She went to open the door. A large bouquet of daisies was thrust at her by Mike.

'Hi there, you. Can I come in?'

'Yes, of course. Please, do come in. Why the flowers?'

'I felt like it. I saw them at a stand at the station and thought you might like them. I'm completely free this evening. Do you fancy doing something?'

'I'm in a mess. Let me clear up a bit.'

'You're not kidding, are you? Do you always work like this?'

'Not always. Quite often though. What do you want to do?'

'Pictures? Drink? Meal out somewhere?'

'Yes please. It all sounds lovely. Hang on a mo. If I just collect those pages and put them up on the desk. The books can be shuffled together. Oh, that's just rubbish. I'll put that out for recycling.' Five minutes sorting and she was clearer once more. 'That's better. Sorry, do sit down.'

'I was wondering when you were going to suggest that,' he laughed. 'Come and sit with me.' He leaned over and kissed her. 'I've missed you. The party on Boxing Day was incredibly boring. I had a rotten time and wished I was still with you. I've been working at the factory ever since. This is the first moment I've really had to myself. So, coming to see you was perfectly natural.'

'I'm glad to see you. If you'd let me know, I'd have been ready for you. But not to worry. What do you want to do?'

'How about a drink and then some dinner? I know a nice pub not too far away. Only trouble is, I'm on my bike. Solution: you ride pillion, you drive, we get a taxi. What do you think?'

'I can always drive. I really don't mind. It all sounds good to me.'

'Decision made. You can drive me to wherever I want to go.' She frowned.

'Not just anywhere, thanks very much. I want feeding and pampering if I'm driving.'

'Very well. Are you going like that or are you planning to change?'

'I s'pose I'd better change. Mind you, grunge is good. Everyone says so, you know.'

'No fiancée of mine goes out looking

like a . . . well, never mind.'

'Oh yes. I'm your fiancée again, aren't I?'

'I have a ring for you to practise wearing. If you're sure you really don't mind.'

'I don't think I mind too much. In fact, I quite like the idea. I really don't know why it's so important to you though.'

'Like I said, it's a matter of being independent. I'll explain it more sometime soon, I promise. Here it is: the dreaded ring.' He took out a small box and handed it to her. Inside was a pretty ring with a garnet stone in it. She looked at it and at him.

'Where did you get this from?' she asked.

'It's an old one given to me by my grandma. My sister also had a few bits but this one was for me. I doubt it's terribly valuable, but it will do nicely for this particular cause.'

'It's lovely. I really like it. I'll wear it for you for however long you want me to.'

'That's very good of you. Thank you. Now, what are we going to do?'

'I've got a pizza in the freezer. Would you like some of that? Then we can go out and see a film?'

'Sounds excellent. I'll admit, I could easily eat a horse or two. We can go and eat somewhere if you'd prefer to?'

'No problems. I can easily cook this, if you can trust my cooking of course.' She went into the kitchen, retrieved the pizza and put it in the oven. She checked carefully that she had put the correct switches on this time.

Mike was reading some of her notes when she went back into the lounge. She sat on the arm of his chair and looked over his shoulder.

'Do you understand what I'm getting at?' she asked.

'I think so. It's all a continuation to what you were teaching before Christmas, isn't it? I recognise the concept.'

'Yes, indeed it is. But please, put it down now or you won't want to listen to my lectures next term.'

'You're just too clever, aren't you?'

'I'm bright but nothing too clever at all. It's my subject and I know it well, that's all.'

'Why would you really want to spend time with me?'

'Why wouldn't I? You're bright. You're handsome. You're talented in many ways.'

'I'm not really bright. Not compared to you. You're lovely and clever and you know what you're talking about. For goodness sake, I go and keep women company for money. All so that I can remain independent.'

'I really don't understand this fanaticism you have for independence. I mean to say, you moved out of your parents' house for whatever reason and you have a good life. I know you earn pretty well from your escort duties.'

'I don't get all of what it costs, you realise.'

'I know you don't, but you get a fair bit. What are you saving for?'

'I'll tell you one day soon. Now, how

is that pizza doing do you think? I don't fancy another burnt offering, much as I love brown food.'

Joanne went into the kitchen and took salad stuff from the fridge and managed to make two bowls of reasonable salad. They needed some-thing extra with just one pizza between them. She knew about his appetite and wanted to make sure he had enough. The pizza smelt good and was perfectly cooked. She put it on the two plates and called him into the kitchen.

'I hope you don't mind eating in here. There isn't a huge amount of room but it's quicker than moving everything in there.'

'This looks wonderful,' he told her as he sat down. 'Salad too? You're spoiling me.'

'Someone needs to. You don't look after yourself properly. You were going to take me out without eating anything, weren't you?'

'I dare say we'd have found a snack or two from somewhere.'

They ate in silence for a few minutes and then he said:

'I like your style of cooking. This is my idea of heaven on a plate.'

'Glad you're liking it. So, tell me what you've been doing with your week.'

'I'm trying to implement a new system into the factory's position. It's a bit tricky. I'll ask you about it after New Year if I may.'

'Course you can. I'd be glad to help out if I can.'

'That would be terrific. I know it's almost there but there are a few snags still. Now, if you've finished, shall we go out?'

'Okay. I'll just pop up and change. Can't have you let down by a scruffy woman with you.'

6

Mike arrived at her house at ten o'clock on New Year's Eve. She was dressed in jeans and a baggy shirt, ready to spend the day working.

'You look good enough to eat,' Mike announced.

'I don't know what you mean, kind sir,' she said. He came inside and kissed her, lifting her off her feet and swinging her round. 'Steady on,' she said, laughing as they both collapsed onto the sofa. He kissed her a lot more and she felt as if this was going to be the start of something much bigger.

'Are you wearing my ring?' he asked, lifting her hand to look. 'Oh yes, you are. That's good.'

'Why?'

'Don't be silly. You know why.'

'Oh yes. Independence. I still think there's a lot more to it. But hey, ours not to reason why. Let's go, shall we?'

They went to his father's workshop and she met his parents for the first time. He introduced her as his fiancée and his mother positively wept.

'Oh my dear,' she said. 'I never thought this day would come. I'm so thrilled and I know you're going to be made very welcome into our family.'

'Well, thank you, Mrs Thomas. It's lovely to meet you too.' She felt mortified that it was all a big pretence. She glared at Mike for putting her into this situation. His father was also pleased but made a little less fuss about it.

'We should celebrate. Go and fetch one of the bottles of bubbly, dear. We need to welcome Joanne to the family properly.'

'Oh please, don't worry on my account. I'm here to work for the day. Help you get things ready for the big party this evening.'

'Don't be silly. We need to give you a proper welcome to the family.' Obediently, Mr Thomas went off to find a bottle. 'Now tell us all about yourself. Mike says you work at the college. Are your parents still around? Oh, of course they are. Mike said you went there for Christmas. Tell me, dear, are your parents thrilled with the news?'

'Well, they don't actually know about it yet,' she blustered.

'Why don't you ring them and invite them over for the evening? I must say, I can't wait to meet them. A lovely girl like you, your parents must be equally lovely.'

'I'm afraid they had plans for today,' Joanne muttered, looking desperately at Mike for his support. This was getting out of control.

'Yes, they're going to a party tonight,' he said feebly.

'Excuse me for moment. I need the loo,' she said. 'P'raps you can show me where to go?'

'Of course. Come through here.'

'Why on earth did you put me in this position?' she demanded. 'It is ridiculous. Your parents are already planning the wedding, for heaven's sake. I really hate lying to them. They seem so lovely.'

'Well, that's a start,' he replied. 'If you hated them, it would be so much easier.'

'Why on earth would I hate them?'

'Oh forget it. Please, just play along with them. We'll talk about it all later. If you really hate me, I shall understand. Look, I really don't want them finding out about my escort duties. This is another reason for this charade. I didn't know they were going to be quite so over the top about it all. I'm really sorry.'

'Oh heavens. How on earth are we going to cope with the rest of this day? They're going to announce it to everyone.'

'I'll have a word. Say we don't want it made public until we've told your parents. Will that do for you?'

'Go and do it now, while I'm on the loo.'

He left her there. She stood for a moment or two and then went back.

She smiled at Mike's parents and said she hoped they could understand.

'Very well, dear,' his mother said.

'So are we going to drink this now or leave it till later?' Mr Thomas asked.

'I say let's have it now,' Mike chipped in.

'Sounds good to me.' His father opened the bottle and poured four glasses. 'Cheers and congratulations,' he said.

Mike stood beside Joanne, his arm laid across her back. She raised her glass to the others and drank.

'What's going here?' said a voice from the doorway. 'Am I missing something?'

'Sally. Come on and have a drink with us,' Mr Thomas said cheerfully. 'We're just wishing success to ourselves for this evening.' Joanne smiled at him. He was clearly a tactful man and had appreciated the scene right away.

'I'll tell you later,' his wife said with a wink.

'I'm Joanne, Mike's girlfriend,' she said, holding out her hand. She was planning to remove the ring from her third finger as soon as possible.

'Pleased to meet you. Sally. I work here but I doubt Mike has mentioned me at all.'

'Of course he's mentioned you. Said how much you keep things moving around here,' she lied.

'That's something. He usually never mentions anyone in this family. Independent or what?' Joanne laughed.

'Typical man.'

They soon finished the drinks and set to work. There was a large area to be cleared of bits and pieces of equipment and stores to be settled on one side. It was quite a room. They all worked hard to move stuff and then to decorate the place with a series of flags and balloons. Joanne and Mike worked together and ended up laughing like crazy over blowing up balloons.

'Come on you two. There are some sandwiches to eat through here. I hope you like smoked salmon, Joanne? It's Mike's favourite.'

'Yes, I remember that. He ate like it was going out of fashion one evening at my place.'

'Where do you live?' asked Sally.

'Over the park in a side street.'

'Not one of those newish places?'

'Yes. I moved there about three years ago.'

'How lovely. You must be earning pretty well to afford one of those.'

'I'm a lecturer, so not too bad. You work here don't you?'

'For my sins, yes I do. As does Mike of course. How long have you two been going out?'

'Not very long, actually.'

'Really? You seem very tuned in together. I've been married for ages but we don't seem to get on as well as you two. He'll be here later, so let me know what you think. He's home with the kids for now.'

'I'm not sure I could say after such a brief meeting.' She took what Mike's sister said very seriously.

'Don't worry. I won't hold you to

anything.' She was laughing as she spoke. 'I was only joking, you realise. Now, what else do you want me to do?' she asked her mother, while Joanne stood blushing at her stupid remark.

'I'm going home in a minute or two. I've got several crates of food ready to bring over. It's going to be tricky to get them into my car so can you come to help me?'

'No rest for the wicked. I'll see you later. Happy balloon blowing.' Sally breezed off after her mother.

'She's nice,' Joanne told Mike. 'I really like her. You're all pretty nice and this is exactly why I don't like cheating on them. I'm taking the ring off for a while. If we can keep a lid on being engaged for the rest of the day, I shall be delighted.'

'Okay. If you insist. I think the parents were happy enough about it though.'

'I do insist. I don't want it getting to my parents for many moons yet. If ever.'

'Look, I'm really sorry I put you through this. Maybe it was a mistake, I admit that. But really, I'd like to be engaged to you but I can't. I'll tell you about it at some point but not for a while yet. Now, balloon blowing, Miss Swithenbank. Only fifty more to go.'

By four o'clock the room was transformed. It looked very different from the place they'd all seen first thing. It had a proper party atmosphere and didn't look like a workshop at all.

'This is exactly what I'd hoped for,' Mrs Thomas said happily. 'Perfect. You were quite right, Mike. You said we could do it and you've made it all happen. What do you think, dear?'

'Looks okay I s'pose.' Mike's father was clearly not a man of many words. He perked up at his wife's expression. 'Very nice indeed. I only hope you'll be here tomorrow to un-decorate it all. We have to work again once this weekend is over and done.'

'I can come over tomorrow,' offered Joanne.

'Thank you my dear. Very good of you.'

'I'm just not sure where we will put all the balloons,' she smiled. 'I suppose we might pop them first.'

'I doubt there'll be very few left. You haven't met our balloon-popping side of the family yet,' Mike said with a laugh. 'This year is a very much larger party than usual. There are a whole load of Aussies over. They have been in the area for a couple of days, causing chaos no doubt.'

'They're family members?'

'They belong to my father's side. Six of them. My father's brother and wife and four younger folk. We met them last night and they're pretty riotous.'

'Should be fun tonight then. Now, if you can take me home, I'd like to get myself ready.'

'Okay. I suspect there's nothing much more to be done here. You brought the music over this morning, didn't you, Dad?'

'What music?'

'All the stuff I recorded over the last week and a half.'

'So where is it?'

'On my iPod. Oh, don't worry. I'll sort it later. Honestly, do it yourself or miss it out,' he grumbled as they were leaving. 'Thanks very much for all your help anyway. You worked hard all day. Hope you're not too weary now?'

'I'm fine. Thanks for asking. I'll have a bath and that will soon sort me out. Are you coming back to fetch me or should I drive myself?'

'Of course I'll fetch you. Good thing I got the car to myself for the day. Mel's gone away for the holiday so it's all mine.'

'I see. Must be inconvenient to have to manage without it being permanently there when you need it.'

'We manage. Bit of give and take. Okay. I'll pick you up at what, seven?'

'When are the rest of the world arriving?'

'About eightish I think. I just wanted some time alone with you first.' She felt a thrill run through her. She was looking forward to this evening, but the idea of a bit of time spent together first pleased her no end.'

She lay in her bath a while later, thinking of him with great pleasure. What was it he'd said about them being properly engaged? He'd like it very much but couldn't for a while. Why not? she wondered. Was it her? Was it some other deeper reason? All a bit strange. She did, however, know one thing. She was in love with this man. One way or another, he'd got into her soul. She would try to control her feelings and wait for him to come round to her way of thinking. She closed her eyes and thought about him a whole lot more. His dark hair, blue eyes and his almost perfect good looks. He was quite a bit taller than she was, but with heels it was perfect. At least she was spending a fairly important evening of the year with him. He wasn't escorting some expensively dressed floozy to a party somewhere. He was all hers for the night. Well, for a long evening, anyway. She had better not count her chickens about the whole night! She shivered suddenly. Sleeping with Mike? It certainly frightened her and hopefully, by the time it really happened, she'd be over it. She got out of the bath and dried herself. She took out her silver dress from the wardrobe and slipped it on. Immediately she looked to see a different girl in her mirror. She would do for Mike. She twisted her hair into its knot and put on some make up. She was ready. And it was only six-fifty.

It was seven-fifteen by the time Mike was knocking at her door.

'I'm so sorry to be late. I had a few problems in getting the sound system working. It all seems okay now though. I say; you look amazing. I really love that dress. It suits you beautifully.'

'Thank you. You're very kind.'

'I really mean it. It's perfect on you.' He reached over to her and took her in his arms. 'I really can't believe you're coming with me to what is just a family

117

party.' Holding her close to him, he kissed her and sent all her senses soaring into space. She looked up at him, saying:

'Thank you for inviting me. I can hardly believe it either. I'm looking forward to it. You're looking pretty smart yourself.'

'Thank you. Shall we go then?'

'Okay. I'm ready to meet the rest of your family. Fiancée or not.'

'I'm sorry. But let's forget about all of that for now. Let's go.'

The room was still empty of people, except for Mike's parents. They had changed and looked very smart.

'Oh my word. Don't you look lovely?' Mrs Thomas said. 'I can really see why he was so attracted to you. Okay, I know. I mustn't say anything on that score. But you do look really lovely my dear.'

'Thank you very much,' Joanne said softly. 'You're looking lovely too.'

'So who's this you've brought with you?' Mr Thomas asked his son. 'Surely she isn't with you?'

'Okay, Dad. Cut it out.'

'I wondered how anyone looking like this could come with you. Please may I have a dance later? I can put you right about this young man; tell you stuff about him that will put you off him forever.'

'Thanks. I'd like that. I need some information about this son of yours.'

Very soon, the room began to fill with family and friends. The Aussie contingent arrived amidst a great noise. Joanne was surprised to see them all arriving with sound waves that would have disturbed anyone's peace. She was introduced to them all and met with their approval.

'Why any dingbat like old Mike should attract a fancy bird like you is beyond me,' said one of them. 'If you want someone to really show you what's what, call on me.' She laughed and promised she would. 'So you gonna come and strut your stuff with me?'

'I should think so. Thanks for asking.'

For the following half hour she was dancing solidly with one then another of Mike's Aussie relatives. Dancing was maybe a rather loose term but she enjoyed herself and hardly stopped laughing the whole time. She went to the bar for something to drink and Mike immediately came to join her.

'Are you all right?' he asked. 'Need saving from the rellies? I gather that's what I have to call them. You know, Aussie style.'

'I'm fine actually, thanks. That Jacob is quite a character, isn't he?'

'I suppose so. I didn't like the way he commandeered you though.'

'Jealous, are we?'

'Naturally. I want you all to myself.'

'Sorry. You can have me for at least the next five minutes.'

'Thanks a bunch,' he laughed. 'Come and dance with me then.'

'Let me finish my orange juice and I'll be right there.'

She finished it and they went to dance. Luckily, it was a slower number and she snuggled close to him. They smooched their way round the floor and ended standing still, a million miles away from the party.

'I love you, Mike Thomas,' she whispered so quietly that he didn't hear her.

'What did you say?'

'Nothing. Just how much I enjoyed that dance.'

'Me too. I could dance with you forever and still have room for more.'

'How romantic,' she whispered.

The party went on till almost midnight. At which point, Mr Thomas called on everyone to make sure they had something in a glass to toast the New Year.

'Get ready for the countdown,' he instructed. Everyone joined in together and raised their glasses at midnight.

'Kiss me,' Mike said to her. She did.

Various people began to leave once the midnight celebrations were over. The younger ones stayed on and Joanne was asked to dance again by the various family members. For once, she forgot her shyness and enjoyed dancing and whirling round. Mike cut in on the deal and took her hands and danced around with her once more.

'Are you ready to leave?' he asked.

'If you want to. I'm happy with whatever you want to do.'

'I'll take you home then. It is after one o'clock. Time for all good girls to be tucked up in their beds.'

'Hey Mike, you're not ducking out already are you?' Jacob asked him. 'Not taking that lovely woman with you are you?'

'Afraid so. I have to take Joanne back to her home. It's past her bedtime.'

'Aw shucks. I can't believe you actually have a bedtime.'

'Oh believe me, I do.' She was laughing at the innuendo and leaned over to kiss him.

'Thanks. You two make a lovely pair. I guess we'll all be invited back to the wedding before too long.'

'Not for a long time,' Mike informed

him. 'But if we do get married, I promise you'll be on top of the list. You ready, darling?'

'Oh yes. I think so. Bye. It's been great to meet you all.'

'Sorry if I dragged you away,' Mike told her on their way back to her house.

'Not at all. I was ready to leave. I felt I did my bit for Australian/UK relationships.'

'You certainly did. Jacob would have loved to come back home with you. I could see by the way he was coming on to you.'

'I hardly noticed,' she teased him. He looked at her.

'Come off it. You must have noticed.'

'I was teasing you. Of course I noticed. But I wanted to come back home with you. Nobody else. But I'm still not sure I've forgiven you for being sort of engaged to me. It was awful when your parents were so pleased about the whole business.'

'It never occurred to me that they would be so pleased. I just wanted them to accept it and not make any fuss. I'm sorry it didn't work out like that.'

'I'll give you the ring back when we get home. Don't let me forget it, will you?'

'Keep it for a while. They'll be sure to invite you round again soon. Let them believe in this fantasy for a while at least.'

'You really are a very strange man. I really don't understand you.'

'Shut up.' He stopped the car outside her house. 'Come here, woman.' He leaned over and kissed her once more. She shut up for all of five minutes.

'Do you want a coffee?' she asked him when she resurfaced.

'Wouldn't say no.'

'Come on in then. And please, behave yourself. This is a quiet street,' she giggled.

He followed her to the door and waited to be let in. They went into the sitting room and sat down on the comfy sofa.

'Coffee?' he asked.

'Sorry. Yes of course. I'll go and make it.'

'I'll come with you. Can't trust you with the coffee pot on your own.' He followed her into the kitchen and stood close to her as she put on the kettle. 'Know something? I don't really want any coffee after all.' He caught her into his arms and, once more, the world stopped turning. They snuggled together on the sofa until both were nearly falling asleep.

'I think I should leave you now. I'll come back tomorrow to collect you for the undressing of the workshop, if you're sure you want to be a part of it?'

'Of course I do. I want to be with you as much as I can during the holiday.'

'It's so late now. I'll see you tomorrow.'

'Bye Mike.' He drove off and she was left yawning and reflecting on a splendid evening. 'I hope you'll sleep with me soon now,' she whispered to the wind.

7

It really had been a lovely evening, Joanne thought when she awoke the next morning. She glanced at her clock. She shot out of bed in horror. It was already ten-thirty. Mike had agreed to come and fetch her at eleven to sort out the room. She went into the shower and dressed quickly. Breakfast? No time, she thought. She did make some coffee and was halfway through drinking it when Mike arrived.

'Do you want some coffee?' she asked him immediately.

'No thanks. I had some before I left. I'm a bit late again. Sorry.'

'I didn't even wake up till ten-thirty,' she confessed.

'Disgraceful. I didn't either.'

In the factory rooms it was still chaotic. There were balloons deflating all over the place and rubbish collected in one corner in a heap. Mike's parents were there, sweeping things together and collecting the flags from round the room.

'What can I do?' she asked.

'If you could stuff some of the rubbish into the bags, that would be great.'

'I'll find the bags. We'll work on this between us,' Mike offered. He fetched a heap of black sacks and they began to fill them. 'How so few people could make so much rubbish beats me.' They stuffed the sacks and made short work of the balloons, stamping on them and reducing them to tiny bits of rubber. It was all rather silly and giggly. 'I think we make a good team,' he said as they finished the tasks.

'I want to get the machines back into their places. Can you manage to help with that?' Mr Thomas suggested. They were all on wheels, so it was a simple matter. 'Heavens, you can certainly work hard, my dear,' he told her.

'Nice to be able to help. Is there anything else?'

'I think that's about it. You are coming back for lunch, aren't you?'

'I, er . . . I don't know,' she replied.

'We thought we'd eat back at Jo's place,' Mike told him.

'Nonsense. Your mother's busily cooking enough food to feed an army. Get yourselves over there right away. She's waiting for you.'

'But . . . ' began Mike.

'Get over there. We won't take no for an answer.'

'See what they're like? I did warn you,' Mike said with a wry grin.

'Okay. Thanks. We'll enjoy some nice food. Must be better than my efforts at cooking.'

'This is true. Okay Dad. See you back at home.'

They drove along the lanes and were soon at the Thomases' house. In the large drive, there were several cars parked.

'Looks as if they have other folks

there,' Joanne remarked.

'I suspect it's the Aussie contingent again. Hope you can cope with Jacob's flirting with you all over again. I'm not exactly sure I can.'

'Oh dear, I'm really scruffy. I should have put on something a bit smarter.'

'Rubbish. You look lovely to me.'

'You're prejudiced,' she told him. 'You have no idea how people should look when invited out for Sunday lunch.'

'It isn't even Sunday. Come on then. Let's go and face the crowd. But we won't stay all afternoon. We'll get off soon after we've eaten. I want you to myself for a bit.' She smiled at him and nodded her head.

As it turned out, Mike was asked to play the piano for everyone to have a sing-song. It was fun and they all enjoyed themselves. Someone over-heard her singing and asked her to sing alone.

'I'm not sure what I can sing,' she said, feeling rather shy. 'I'd really rather not, actually.'

'Mike, you sing with her. You've got a good voice.'

'Okay. Give us a minute.' They chatted quietly and decided to sing something from the charts they both knew. 'Okay everyone. This is from last year's charts. With suitable apologies to Declan.' After a false start, they soon got the number going properly and sang the words without hesitating. There was great applause all round and calls for more.

'Sorry,' Mike said. 'But we really have to go now. It's been great to see you all again.' They made their farewells and Mike's parents had a special word with her in their hall.

'Do come and see us again soon. It's been lovely to meet you and I just know you two are right for each other. We can do some wedding planning when you come round.'

'Thanks, Mrs Thomas, but it's going to be a very long time before we get married.'

'Let's just see, shall we?'

'Goodbye and thank you very much for a delicious lunch. I really enjoyed it.'

'Bye, Mum and Dad. I'll see you later during the week or something.'

They left, driving back through the country lanes. Soon they were back at Joanne's home and he stopped outside.

'Am I invited in?' he asked.

'Course you are. Don't you have to be somewhere though?'

'Well, not really. I'd love to spend an evening alone with you. If you don't mind too much.'

'I'd be delighted. I was only going to watch television. A DVD or something.'

'That sounds great. A nice quiet evening, just you and a DVD. Perfect.'

They went inside and soon settled down in front of the television.

'I'm not sure what sort of thing you'd like? Romantic fiction is my cup of tea but there are several different ones you can choose from.' He actually chose one of her favourites so she was very happy. They cuddled close together on the sofa to watch it and both of them finally fell asleep. He woke up and jumped.

'Where am I?' he asked. 'Oh yes. A nice movie and look at me, I fall asleep.'

'Less chat please,' Joanne managed to mutter.

'Shall I make us a coffee?'

'Okay. If you must move.' She flopped over to lie down and waited for him to sort out the coffee. She almost fell asleep again.

'Come on, you. Coffee, and I found some crackers and cheese. Thought you may need a snack to keep you going.'

'You're incorrigible aren't you? Never can eat enough.' She sat up smiling at him. 'How on earth did your Mum ever manage with you?'

'She managed pretty well really. She only does a bit of work for the company in extremis. Not that it happens very often these days.' He looked pretty dismal and sighed rather a lot.

'What's wrong?' she asked him.

'Oh, you know. You don't really want to hear about it. Shall we watch something else?'

'I'd rather hear what's bugging you.'

'It's just that . . . well, Dad doesn't seem to want to listen to us. Sally and I just know that unless we try to expand the business, we're going to go down the pan.'

'But he seemed a pretty decent guy, your father. Why wouldn't he want to expand the business, for goodness sake?'

'He's afraid that any further investment would be lost. Money wasted. Meantime, I'm out and about all the time trying to get new orders and trying to make things work out properly. We're not in the total doldrums, but we need the system updating and the pay structure is pathetic anyway. I don't get nearly enough for what I want to do, and have to put up with it. Hence the escort agency.'

She listened to him moaning and gave thought to anything they could do to improve his situation.

'I can look over your computer stuff. See if there's anything that I can suggest. I've got another few days before college starts again and so there's plenty of time.'

'Would you really? That would be terrific. We're back tomorrow anyway so it would be great if you came in with me. I don't know quite what Dad has in mind to do tomorrow, but I'm sure I can give you some time.'

'Okay. Do we need to tell him I'm coming in?'

'Not at all. He won't like you seeing all our stuff, but it's desperate times ahead I'm afraid.'

They ate some cheese and drank the coffee, talking through the plans for the next day. It all sounded rather complex and she hoped she would be able to offer some solution at least.

'You know something? I feel shattered. Do you mind going now?' Joanne told him.

'Not at all. I feel shattered too. All been a bit much lately. Too many parties and too many late nights.'

'All right for some,' she laughed. 'I've

134

only had a couple of late nights.'

'Okay. I take your point. I'll collect you in the morning. Oh no, Mel's back tonight. He'll be sure to want the car. Do you mind driving to the factory? I can cycle there as usual.'

'Not a problem. I could pick you up if you wanted.'

'No, it's probably best if I cycle there. Then you can leave whenever. You don't want to be stuck there with me all day.'

'Okay. I'll look forward to seeing you tomorrow.' They kissed goodnight and he drove away.

Joanne washed up their dishes and mugs and sat down again. What had she offered to do? It wasn't such a good plan, she realised. It meant assimilating all their work problems and then trying to sort it all out immediately. It would be a terrific job and she would probably have to suggest all sorts of things they wouldn't like. Still, she had made an offer and she needed to fulfill it. She went to bed and settled down for a good night's sleep. Unfortunately, her mind continued to worry over the factory and everything it might entail. She slept a little but awoke again and worried some more.

She gave up at six o'clock and got up. She didn't even know what time they began to work. She hit on nine o'clock as a reasonable time and planned to arrive then. She pottered round the house, cleaning and tidying the already tidy place, all the time worrying about what she was going to find at the factory. She didn't even know exactly what they made there or who else worked at the place.

She drove to the factory and parked outside. There were only two other cars parked, one being Mr Thomas's and, presumably, the other belonging to Sally. There was also a bicycle she assumed belonged to Mike. She felt her heart thud at the thought of him being there. She swallowed hard and pushed open the door.

'Hallo?' she called. 'Anyone around?'

'Oh Joanne. Come in. I'm afraid you've had a wasted journey but it's very nice to see you.' Mr Thomas was wearing a brown coat and looked as if he was in the middle of doing something.

'I'm here at Mike's request. He felt there may be something I might suggest to improve the computer system?'

'Very good of you but I think we're all fine.'

'Okay. May I see Mike for a moment then?'

'We're just having a family meeting actually.'

'Very well, I'll disappear then. Sorry to trouble you.' She turned to leave, feeling somewhat snubbed.

'Joanne, hi. Come on through.' It was Mike with quite a different attitude.

'Morning, Mike,' she said politely. 'Your father says there's nothing I can do to help. I was just about to leave.'

'Rubbish. Come on through. I think you need to know the situation from the inside.'

'Mike, don't start again.' His father

137

looked so angry, Joanne was afraid he was about to start shouting. She had never wanted to be on the inside of such an event.

'Don't worry, Mike. I can come back at another time. I don't want to be in the way.'

'Let her go, Mike. She doesn't want to be involved in our family affairs. Not until after you're married.'

She went to the door and Mike followed her. He came outside with her and spoke angrily.

'You can see what he's like. He doesn't want to admit that we're going down the pan. Sally and I were just telling him the situation but he doesn't want to listen. Honestly, I feel like looking for another job somewhere.'

'Don't do anything too rash. It wouldn't make sense to crash out of his life like that.'

'Well, honestly, he takes the biscuit. If only he'd listen to my suggestions. It would make all the difference to the business.'

'You go back to your meeting. I'll see you sometime later shall I?'

'Indeed you will. I'll call you. And Jo, thanks very much for coming. I'm only too sorry that you were treated so badly.'

'I really don't mind. Back to my own work for the rest of the day.'

As she drove back, she thought about the system at the factory. By system, she reflected, he meant the staffing. If it really was just the three of them, they were all a bit too close. They clearly didn't have any orders for whatever they were making. It was a large room with plenty of space. She would ask Mike more about it when he came round later. Would he arrive that evening? If he did, he would need feeding. She diverted to the supermarket and made a few purchases. 'Just in case' types of things. She now had a free day. What might she do with it? She parked the car and went into the High Street to look at the shops. The sales were in full swing so she went into several clothes shops and perused their stocks. She picked up one or two things and went to try them. Not quite her usual style, but she liked them and decided to buy them.

'Joanne, what are you doing here? Not your usual place to be buying stuff.' It was Trisha.

'No, I know it isn't, but I decided to look into buying something. What do you think?' She opened her bag for her friend to look inside.

'Nice colour. I like it. Have you time for a coffee?'

'Why not? Where shall we go?'

'There's a nice place here. Come on. My treat.'

They went up to the top floor, where the coffee bar was situated. It was quite busy but they found a table and were soon drinking steaming hot cappuccinos.

'So, how was Christmas? Oh, and New Year too?'

'Really good, thanks. How about yours?'

'I finished with my chap at New Year. Bit of a blow really but we were going nowhere fast. How's the gorgeous Mike?'

'He is just that. Still gorgeous.'

'The real thing, gorgeous?'

'I think so.'

'Did you ask him about the woman I saw him with?'

'She was a family friend. Someone who asked him to make up the numbers, I gathered.'

'He seemed pretty keen on her. Well, we thought so, anyway.'

'So, tell me what happened to you and Dave? I thought it was about to be an engagement or at least moving in together. You've been around together for quite some time haven't you?'

'Almost two years. I don't want to talk about it though. All a bit new and raw at present. It ended on New Year's Eve. A huge big row and bam, that was it. Tell me about your times? Cheer me up a bit.'

For the next half hour, they chatted

about their men friends and Joanne realised that Trisha and her fellow were really only having a temporary break. They'd had a blistering row and walked out on each other. Trisha kept on talking about him, despite her words that she didn't need anyone. At last they decided to leave and Joanne breathed a sigh of relief. Trisha in this sort of mood was difficult to handle.

'I'd better go now. Stuff to do.'

'When are you seeing Mike again?' she asked.

'This evening probably. Haven't fixed anything yet. I have a load of work to get through in the meantime.'

'I was wondering if I could come round for a bit more therapy?' Trisha asked.

'Well, okay. Now, do you mean?'

'Well, yes. If it's not too much trouble.' She looked so sad and woebegone, Joanne didn't have the heart to refuse her.

'Okay. I presume you've got your car parked somewhere?'

'Yes. I'll collect it and follow you home.'

As she drove home, Joanne wondered what she'd done. She felt as if she had problems of her own to think through and here she was, suffering a friend with a broken heart. Still, it was the least she could do. Mike's problems with his father would just have to wait. They spent a couple of hours together, with Trisha talking about the horrors of men and her listening, or perhaps half listening.

'You've either got to see him again and talk it through or forget him. That's how it strikes me anyway.' She felt exasperated with her friend and wanted to get on with thinking her own thoughts.

'I'm sorry. I shall have to do as you say. I'll call him and we'll talk it through. I'm sure we'll be back together again soon. I'll get out of your way now. You're obviously a very happy bunny and want to do your own thing.'

'No, wait Trisha. I don't want you to

go when you're so miserable. I'll make a new pot of coffee and some sandwiches.'

'If you're absolutely certain?' Joanne nodded. 'Then thanks a lot. I'd really appreciate it. You're a true friend.'

'I can but try.'

It was after four o'clock by the time Trisha was ready to leave. She had wept, laughed, and finally giggled.

'Thanks so much. I do feel so much better now. You were just what I needed. Bye then.' She gave her friend a hug and set off for her own home.

Joanne felt exhausted. Nothing like listening to a friend berating everyone she'd ever known. Her next problem was going to be sorting out Mike and his problems. Was she up to it? She had no idea. Nor did she have any idea whether he would come round to see her that evening. She had put the food she'd bought away in the fridge and now had a couple of hours to wait to see if he would arrive. She slumped down in front of the television and promptly fell asleep. It was a banging on her door that finally roused her. She went to open it.

'Am I allowed in?' asked Mike.

'Course. Come on. How are you?'

'I'm so fed up I could scream. First of all, let me say how sorry I am for putting you through all of that this morning.' She gave a shrug. 'You can see what we're up against. My father is probably the most pig-headed, unmoveable man in the entire world. He won't even acknowledge the problems exist. He keeps saying that everything will get better in the end. He doesn't realise we're nearly *at* the end.'

'I'll open some wine. You seem in need of it.'

'And then to turn you away like that. It was so rude and unforgivable. I do apologise again.'

'It's okay. Calm yourself down. It just isn't worth it. Here,' she said offering him the glass.

'Thanks. Just what I needed. So tell me, exactly what is the problem?'

'He just doesn't want to listen either to me or Sally. We both realised that things were not going well before Christmas. He didn't want to spoil anything. 'Mustn't upset your Mother' was all we kept hearing.'

'And the New Year's Eve party? Could they actually afford it?'

'Not at all. We suggested cancelling but he wouldn't listen.'

'I wouldn't have drunk so much if I'd known.'

'Don't be silly. No, we decided on using the factory rooms to save hiring the village hall. Not that it was free anyway. They'd had someone else book it in the meantime. You know what I think? I'm going to look for another job. Definitely. I'll pick up a paper and look for something.'

'Okay. If that's what you think is right. Now, would you like some dinner?'

'What have you got?'

'I've got some chili, ready-made, and there's some salad.'

'Sounds like a deal. Thanks very much. Oh, I'm afraid I'm out tomorrow. Another escort duty. I'm sorry.' She pulled a face but would say no more. She really hated it when he took someone else out.

It was quite a pleasant evening. The chili worked well and she got her catering confidence back. They chatted endlessly about his work until there was nothing more to say.

'Come here,' he said softly. 'We've talked about everything there is to talk about. I really want you, you know.'

'Oh Mike, I want you too. But, there's something you should know about me.' She felt almost ready to admit to being a virgin but still quailed at the thought.

'There's nothing you could tell me that could alter how I feel right now.' He kissed her till her senses were reeling. She felt strangely outside her own body and wanted him as she'd never wanted anyone before. 'What do you think?' he asked her again.

'Let's go to bed,' she managed to whisper. He quickly rose and pulled her with him. She remembered the sheets weren't fresh and hesitated. Hang it. They wouldn't be fresh for long even if she'd changed them earlier.

'Come on then. Show me your bedroom.'

8

The pair of them went upstairs and, shyly, she took him into her room. It was at least tidy, she thought.

'This is very nice,' he told her. 'I like the way you've got it. Feminine but not too itsy-bitsy.'

'Thank you.' She hesitated again. Was this what she really wanted?

'What is it?' he asked anxiously.

'I'm just not sure.'

'We don't have to if you don't want to.'

'I'm . . . oh hang it. Come here.' She pulled him closer to him and they kissed once more. She felt him moving to remove her top and allowed him to. He touched her breasts and kissed them, sending her flying into space. 'Oh Mike,' she whispered.

'You like that?' he asked.

'Oh yes.'

He kissed her again and she pulled him closer. Suddenly, it became urgent and they undressed each other with more concentrated efforts. They both stood naked, gazing at each other's bodies in a strange wonder that slowed both of them down.

'You are so lovely,' Mike told her. 'You are perfect.'

'I love your body too. Tall and so straight and so ready for me.'

Gently they lay on her bed and slowly, sensuously he touched her; the urgency had left them both. She lay back, enjoying every moment of his touching and feeling her. Her breasts were erect and almost hurt with the pressure of wanting. He kissed them again and again and she felt almost a burning sensation deep inside. She was helpless and just lay back, loving this man and what he was doing to her. When he rolled on top of her to cover her, she felt as if this was the moment she had been living for all her life. Everything else was forgotten. Her concerns about telling him she was a virgin disappeared, as they made perfect love. A long, slow love-making that lasted for what felt like hours.

★　★　★

'That was sensational,' she managed to murmur some long time later.

'You are so right. Tell me something. Was it really your first time?'

'Why do you ask?' she said, laughing.

'It seemed as if I was entering you for the first time. I don't exactly know why I felt that way but . . . '

'Well, yes it was. I'm sorry.'

'Sorry? Why on earth are you apologising? It was my privilege. Jo, you are a very lovely woman and I was very fortunate to be allowed to be your first. That was quite something.' He lay stroking her some more. 'Was that what you were going to tell me? Before we came upstairs?'

'Well, yes. Was I really all right?'

'Oh Joanne, Joanne. How could you

even think you could disappoint? You are truly amazing. Beautiful. Perfect, in fact. I could never criticise you in any way.'

She grinned up at him, feeling very special.

'Thank you. Are you going to stay the night with me?'

'If I may.'

'Course you can. It simply isn't worth getting up and dressing and going out in the cold, now, is it?'

'Not in the least. Mel would never miss me anyway. I'll need to be up early tomorrow though. We're having yet another meeting in the morning.' He paused, allowing his life to come back into his mind. 'There really isn't much else we can do.'

'No more of that now. Kiss me again. I'm getting to like being in bed with you.'

'Greedy girl. I have to leave you for a moment or two. Don't go anywhere will you?'

He leapt out of bed and went

through to the bathroom. She lay back, thinking that Trisha would never believe all of this. Nor would her parents or anyone else in the family. She smiled to herself, knowing in her heart she had met the man she really wanted to marry. But knowing it was one thing, acting on it was something quite different. She knew it was what she wanted, but he had to know it too. She could not, would not, make any further comment until he did. Was she simply enjoying the sensation of it all? Maybe, but she knew that she loved this man. With all her heart. He came back to bed and they snuggled down together.

The next morning she peered out of the windows.

'Oh goodness. It snowed in the night.'

'Much?'

'Quite a bit, actually. It doesn't look too good for you to cycle to work. I'll get up and drive you there if you like.'

'You know what? I think I'll make it an excuse not to go in. I fancy a day spent together. How do you feel about that?'

'It sounds fabulous. But will your father be all right with you not going in?'

'He can lump it. I think a break from each other will do us all good.'

'I'll go and make some breakfast for us. Bring it up to bed. What do you think?'

'Sounds great. Do you need help?'

'I'm not doing a big bacon breakfast. Toast and coffee okay?'

'Fine. I would never have turned down bacon though.'

'Tough. There isn't any.' She pulled on a dressing gown and went downstairs. It felt cold so she turned up the boiler to heat everywhere a little more. Two more days and she'd be back at college. She made toast and coffee and loaded everything onto a tray. 'Here it comes,' she called as she went up the stairs. He was sitting up in bed, looking gorgeous. She put the tray down and went to kiss him. 'Sorry, I couldn't resist doing that. Budge over and take the tray.'

'What could be better? Sitting up in bed with a beautiful woman eating breakfast while the snow is falling?'

'Nothing, unless it's a beautiful bloke,' she replied. 'That makes it all perfect doesn't it? Hadn't you better phone your father though?'

'I suppose so. I'll do it a bit later though. Don't want him snapping at me to get my butt out there right away.'

'I'm sure we can concoct some dire tale about you being snowed in. Maybe they are snowed in at their house?'

'I doubt it. He'd have called the local snow plough to get him out. Got them all running round to clear the grounds. You don't know my father.'

'Apparently not,' she laughed, getting butter smeared over her chin. He reached over and wiped it off, using one of the neatly laundered napkins she'd put out.

'You do do things nicely,' he told her.

'I like the fact you even put out napkins for us to use.'

'I try to please,' she told him.

'Oh, you certainly know how to please a bloke.'

'I'm glad.'

'Here, let me get rid of this tray,' he said, taking it from her and putting it on the side.

They found things to occupy them both for the next hour or so. She felt so relaxed and happy she didn't know or care what else happened in her life.

'Don't you think you should phone your father now?' she suggested.

'I guess I'd better. Do you mind if I use your phone?'

'Course not. Don't you want to use your mobile?'

'I've left it back at the flat. Silly really but I was so mad when I came over last night. Amazing how things can change isn't it?' He called the office and, getting no response, he phoned his home. It seemed his statements about his father were quite wrong. He was still at home and immediately gave him the day off. 'Now, how good is this? We can stay in bed all day if we want to,' he announced after he'd put the phone down.

'I'd like to stay in for a while but I really do have to do a bit of work. We start back at college in a couple of days.'

'I s'pose I should check with the agency to see if I'm still needed this evening.' It seemed he was. 'I'd better see if I can get back to my flat eventually. I'll have to change and get ready. I s'pose I'll have to get a taxi or something.'

'So where are you off to tonight?' she asked more than a little jealously.

'A dinner or something. I'm not all that sure. I bet it will be cancelled.'

'I hope you find out before you get there. It is still snowing.'

It continued to snow all day. During the afternoon, he tried to get outside but they were well and truly snowed in. He called the agency again and told them he wouldn't be able to go anywhere that evening. They were not pleased and said they'd have to look for someone else to do the job. He eventually put the phone down in quite a bad mood.

'Look, I'm really sorry but it looks as if I'm stuck here indefinitely. Well, until the snow melts at least.'

'That's fine. No worries. I'll do some work tomorrow, whether you're here or not. How about going outside and doing some shovelling? I fancy a bit of fresh air and it has actually stopped for a while.'

'Great. I'd like that.'

They went outside, Mike wearing one of Joanne's older jackets. He had to wear his own shoes, and very soon they were soaking wet. She lobbed a snowball at him and he rolled one of his own and pelted her. Soon they were fighting like mad, both of them weak with laughter.

'Hey, stop now. Please. Look at your bike. It's completely frozen in its little corner.'

'Oh dear, no. I'll have to work on it to thaw it before tomorrow. I promise I will leave tomorrow. Even if I have to walk across the park to my flat.'

'Put it in the garage with my car. There isn't much room but at least it might thaw it a bit. I should have thought of doing it yesterday.'

'Methinks you had other thoughts on your mind yesterday.'

'Perhaps I did. Can you blame me?'

'Not one little bit. I loved it all. Shall we go inside now and light a fire in the lounge? I fancy lying in front of it and making love to you all over again.'

She laughed and led the way back inside. He looked at the fireplace. There was an artificial log burner sitting there. He laughed and cancelled his plans.

'I think it has to be your bed again, darn it.'

She laughed, holding out her freezing hands to him. He took them and kissed them both. They laughed together and he kissed her once more.

'I don't think now is the best time to

go to bed. We need to eat again. I can't have you passing out without any food. I'll have to go and check the freezer. See what's there.'

'You never did get any work done. Do you want to do some now? I can cook and you could work.'

'I doubt it would do me any good really. I'll leave it till tomorrow and do something then. I'll maybe turn you out early enough.'

They spent a pleasant evening, cooking together and watching some television. Neither of them could wait to return to the bedroom. It was becoming a matter of urgency and great appeal to both of them.

The next day, there had been no more snow, so Mike left her after breakfast. He took his bike from the garage and set off, wobbling dangerously. He made much more of it than was really the case, leaving her laughing again. She went back inside and began to sort out her work once more. It seemed a long time since she had done any. So much had happened since those days . . . well, since two days earlier. She smiled to herself, thinking about him lying beside her. She had watched him sleeping at one point and loved the memory of seeing his long eyelashes lying against his cheeks. His rather hairy cheeks. He hadn't shaved for a couple of days and was looking quite outdoorsy and rugged. She hugged herself at the memory. As for her, she was no longer a virgin. It was a very pleasant realisation and she felt happier than she could ever remember. She was now equal to everyone else she knew. With a sigh, she switched on her computer and tried to do something useful.

It was three long days before she saw Mike again. He had phoned her from time to time but had been unable to see her. He told her that he was still fighting with his father, and it was an ongoing situation. She went back to college and was soon back into the swing of things. The snow had cleared quite well and she was still feeling very happy. She was more than ready to see her beloved Mike again when he phoned to ask if she was free that evening.

'There's something I really need to discuss with you.'

'What's that?' Joanne asked.

'I'll tell you when I see you. It's all bit difficult to explain on the phone. I need to be with you to see how you react to what I have to say.'

'Now you've got me really intrigued. What's it all about?'

'I'll tell you when we're together.'

'Shall I organise some dinner?'

'Well, I don't really mind. We can go out somewhere if you'd rather.'

'I'll see. I have some work to finish, but I should get it done fairly soon. I'll see you round sevenish?'

'Okay. I'll be there. Thank you.' He put his phone down and she sat staring at the handset for a second or two. He sounded worried and she felt anxious about whatever it was he was going to ask or tell her. Maybe he had fallen out with his father and wanted to move in with her? What did she think about that idea? Her heart lifted at the prospect but her head was telling her it was much too soon. She frowned. How could she tell him she didn't want him to move in with her if he asked? On the other hand, should she suggest it herself to make it easier for him? Imponderable questions.

9

By the time Mike arrived, she had put together some sort of dinner and felt extremely nervous.

'So what did you want to ask me?' she said almost as soon as he'd taken his coat off.

'Hey, hang on a mo. Let me get inside, won't you?'

'Sorry. I've been worrying ever since you called. Have I done something wrong?'

'Oh Joanne, of course you haven't. My dearest girl, why on earth would you think that?'

'I don't know. I didn't know . . . oh, don't listen to me. If you want to wait for a while, that's fine. Come and have a drink.'

'Just a minute. There's something else I need to do first.' He kissed her and immediately she knew everything would be all right. If he wanted to move in, she'd go for it. Anything he wanted, she'd agree to, as long as he kept kissing her that way. Feeling somewhat misty, they went into the lounge room. The fire was switched on and it all looked very cosy. A new bottle of wine was already opened and waiting on the side. The music was playing softly.

'I'm really sorry I didn't see you yesterday. It has been a difficult couple of days.'

'I'm sorry to hear that,' she told him.

'Mel and I have had a violent row and my father is still being so dammed difficult about everything. He refuses to acknowledge that anything is wrong and doesn't want any changes made. Sally and I spoke to him all day about it. We really need to make a whole raft of changes in the way we are marketed and what we can do for people. The system needs updating — and the way we work. Sorry, it's all a bit raw for me. Oh, thanks a lot,' he said as she gave him some wine.

'I'm really sorry for you. I can't think how it must be for you. Well, for you both, really.'

'Thanks. But there is something I need to ask you.'

'Go ahead. Look, if you want to move in with me, I think it will be all right. I'm not all that certain about it but . . . '

'No, it's nothing like that. The thing is: I've applied for a job in America. They want to see me next weekend. The trouble is, I'm supposed to have a wife and they want to see her at the interview. I suppose you wouldn't consider being my wife, would you?'

'Oh Mike. I'm really not sure. But thank you for asking me. I'd like to, but I still feel we're a little bit new. Sorry, I sound a real wimp, don't I?'

'Not at all. You need to think about it a little.'

'I should know immediately. I'm still getting over the shock of . . . well, everything being so swift.'

'What do you mean?' he asked,

looking puzzled.

'Well, it's only been three weeks or so since we met. Now you're asking me to marry you.'

'Oh, heck, I see. Look, you know how fond of you I am, but I wasn't actually asking you to marry me. I need a wife to take to the interview.'

'You need a wife?' she repeated incredulously.

'I'm so sorry. Yes, and by next week. You wouldn't consider just pretending to be my wife, would you?'

'Good heavens. Not a big ask then.' She tried to come to terms with his request. He'd asked her to pretend to be engaged to him recently and now he was asking her to pretend to be his wife. What was it with him? 'I'll just go and check on dinner.' She just had to get out of his way for a moment. Luckily he didn't follow her. She stood in the kitchen looking at her own reflection. Why did she get into such a mess with someone she went out with? She stirred the pot of sauce and tipped pasta into another pan. She continued to stand by the side of the cooker and wondered what one earth she would say to Mike.

'Are you all right?' he asked, coming into the room. He slipped his arms round her middle from behind her and held her close for several moments. 'Look, I'm so sorry. It was a crazy idea. I should never have asked you.'

'No worries. I'm sort of over the initial shock. I'll think about it and let you know. That feels nice,' she said, turning and snuggling against him. 'I'm glad you weren't really asking me to marry you.'

'Don't worry about it. It's just a stupid idea. I felt that if there was a wife in tow, I'd be more likely to get the darned job in the first place. It's all to do with this business with my father. I want to get a new job just to show him I'm not the useless prat he seems to think I am.'

'Don't be silly. You're not useless and not a prat.'

'Well, listening to him for the last

couple of days, it seems I am to him. Aw, let's forget all about him and this other job. It was just a wacky idea I thought I might manage.'

She turned back to the meal she was cooking and stirred it some more. He leaned over the back of her and dipped a finger into the sauce.

'Mmm. That is so good. What's in it?'

'A couple of frozen frogs I found on the back door step this morning. Onions, herbs and a can of tomatoes. That's about it.'

'Excluding the frogs, I trust.'

'Excluding the frogs, of course.'

'Now, is that food ready to be eaten? If not I'm going to have to take a run round the block.'

'I think it is. Let me test the pasta and if that's done, we have a go situation.'

They ate and drank and talked more about his work. She remembered his comment about Mel and asked what the trouble was there.

'Oh, nothing all that much. He wants

to move his girlfriend in and I said it wasn't acceptable. He threw a wobbly and asked if I was planning to move out. That's why your comment about me moving in here surprised me so much.'

'I hadn't realised it did.'

'I had already wondered about it, but realised that it was all too soon for you. I also realised that I'm your first proper boyfriend and that is also quite some responsibility.'

'I'm glad you see it that way.' She sat back, thinking about him and what he had come to mean to her in so short a time. She already knew she was in love with him, but was it because of the fact that he had been her first lover or because he was truly special? He was truly special, she knew that already. But did she truly love him? Enough to pretend to be his wife?

'Let's go to bed.' He said it quietly and without any emphasis.

'I'd love to, but I do need to wash up and clear the kitchen before morning. I assume you're staying the night?'

'Am I invited to?' he asked cautiously.

'Oh yes indeed. You are expected to stay.' Her words were equally quiet. They went into the kitchen together to wash their plates and the pans. 'You want to wash or dry?'

'I'll wash. Then you can put things away where they go.' As they worked, she realised that they seemed like an old married couple. She loved seeing him standing by the sink and forgot all about drying the dishes. 'So, are you expecting me to dry as well?' he asked after the dishes had built up on the draining board.

'Sorry. I was thinking. Thinking what it would be like having you around much more of the time. I quite like the idea actually.' Soon, it was all clean and tidy. She went up to his back and slipped her arms round his waist. 'Bed now?'

'I should think so. After all, it's already just past nine o'clock. Way past my bedtime.'

'Mine too.' Gently kissing as they went, he led her upstairs to her room. Once there, he undressed her, slowly and gently. When she was naked, he laid her on the bed and began to kiss her whole body. She closed her eyes and lay back, loving the attention. He stopped for a moment to undress himself. She opened her eyes and watched as his body was revealed.

'You are very lovely,' she whispered aloud. 'Of course I'll be your pretend wife.'

'You don't have to agree right now,' he said as he kissed her breasts.

'It's all right. Mmm.' She spoke as he kissed her mouth to quieten her.

Neither of them spoke again for a while. They made slow and gentle love together. It felt wonderful as he entered her once more. She sighed deeply, wanting this feeling of fulfilment to continue forever.

'Did you mean what you said?' he asked some time later.

'When?'

'Oh, I don't know. Some hours ago.'

'About being your pretend wife?' He nodded. 'Yes. I did. You'll have to brief me properly. I need to know what they'll ask me and how you want me to answer.'

'Oh, I will. Does that mean you'll really agree to doing it?' She nodded, still feeling somewhat doubtful. 'Thank you so much, my darling. It's very good of you.'

'I know it is. And if you get the job? What happens then?'

'We'll sort that out later on. I doubt I'll even be offered the job but I want to make the point to my father.'

'I see. Well, if I can help, I will.' They settled down to sleep. When she awoke the next morning, she looked at her sleeping companion. She knew that she really loved him . . . not just a passing fling; she really did want him to ask her to marry him. Having slept on the thought, she knew she wanted to marry him. But she would wait to be asked properly. No way could she ask him.

She leaned over to him and kissed him. One eye opened and he smiled.

'What a delightful way to be woken,' he murmured somewhat sleepily. 'Come here.' She rolled over to him and kissed him again.

'I'm glad you liked being awoken by me. I'm sorry but I have to get up now. I have an early lecture today.'

'Blow lecturing. Come here and . . . '

'Sorry,' she laughed as she got up quickly. 'You'll have to wait. Come on. You don't want to be late yourself, now, do you?'

'You know something? I really don't give a damn. My father can stew in his own juices.'

'You really don't mean that, you know. You need to show him you are still capable of working and doing everything just as you always have.'

'You may be right. Of course you're right. You always will be, won't you?'

'When exactly is this interview to take place?'

'It's on Saturday. In London. I

thought we might go up there on Friday evening. What do you think? It's either then or a very early start on Saturday.'

'I suppose Friday would be sensible. Wow, that's only the day after tomorrow. I need to know what you want me to wear. Give me a whole long lesson on how long we've been married . . . it's quite a commitment. You are absolutely certain this is really what you want?'

'Yes. Well, it would be nice to be wanted even if I don't see it as a realistic thing. They rang me back right away to ask me to the interview.'

'Well, let's give 'em what they want, shall we?'

'They'll book us into a hotel. I have to call them this morning to let them know when we'll be there. I'll make sure I can have the car too. Mind you, the way Mel's been lately, I'm not sure he'll be all that willing to let me have it.'

'There's always mine if necessary. Is this actually the normal way of doing stuff? I mean, are wives usually interviewed for jobs?'

'In the USA they often are. I was a bit tongue-in-cheek when I applied but hey, it's all quite exciting.'

'I'm just curious about what you'll do if you are offered it.'

'Let's see how things pan out, shall we? Now, are you putting that sweater on or going to use it as a cleaning cloth?'

She laughed and pulled it on.

'Come on now. Time you were up and about. Have you got to go back to your place or are you going straight to work?'

'I'll go back to my flat. See how things are with Mel. Do I get some coffee first? And a slice of toast maybe?'

'If you hurry up. Then I have to get off to work. Will you be coming round tonight?'

'I'm sorry but I have an engagement tonight.'

'Oh.'

'Sorry, love. It was a long-term booking made ages back. I can't avoid it I'm afraid.'

'I hope you enjoy it then.' She hated it when he went out on bookings. 'So, I reckon I'll see you on Friday evening then. It takes well over a couple of hours to drive into London. When do you want to make a start?'

'When do you finish at college?'

'I can get away soon after lunchtime if you want.'

'Great. I'll come and collect you from here at two-thirty. How does that suit you?'

'Okay. I'll look forward to seeing you then. I'm not sure how much I'm looking forward to the interview, mind you.'

Joanne worried about what she'd agreed to all through the day. At one point she sat with Trisha, who asked her what was wrong. She didn't tell her.

'So how are things with you and your man?' she asked instead.

'I think we're going to work through it. It isn't easy when you've known each other for so long.'

'Good. That's very good news.' Then

she subsided into another mood of silence and wouldn't be drawn on what was wrong. Whatever she felt about it, she had committed to it now and she had to see it through. But, as she believed she was in love with this man, it wasn't so very difficult.

The following day was a busy one for Joanne and she came home feeling weary. She hadn't arranged anything for the evening and was looking forward to slumping and maybe reading something. She drank some wine when she got home and felt better. She was still worried about her plans for the weekend. What was going to happen when they asked her how long they'd been married? She dreaded to think about the finer details of this pretence. Hang it all, it was a weekend in London with Mike. That was going to be perfect, she was quite determined about that.

He phoned her late in the evening.

'Hi Jo. How are you?' he asked.

'I'm okay, thanks. And you?'

'I'm good. I was wondering if all is okay for tomorrow?'

'I suppose so. I'm not one hundred percent happy about this interview but I suppose you really do know what you're doing?'

'Of course. You can tell them you're a lecturer and will always follow me out there. Then if it doesn't work out, we can tell them you're not able to give up your job. Or, well, something along those lines.'

'Mike?' She was silent for a moment. 'You mean you'll still go? Even if I don't?'

'Let's talk on the way tomorrow. We'll get it all sorted before the interview. We're staying at the Belmont Hotel in Knightsbridge, by the way. It's not the very best but I think it's pretty nice.'

'Great. I'll look forward to it all.'

'I'll be with you by two-thirty tomorrow. Might as well make the most of it all. Okay?'

'Fine,' she told him before putting the phone down.

He was making use of her. She just knew it. He was using her to solve a problem he had with his father and she was just going along with it. Why on earth had she agreed to do it? It was quite ridiculous. She picked up the phone to call him back, but put it down again.

10

By the time Mike came round to collect her, Joanne was ready. She had troubled herself over what to take with her and finally decided on the outfit she had worn for her interview at the college. It was a few years old, but it was timeless and she had never worn it since. She had also packed another dressy outfit in case they went out somewhere exciting. Once she had swallowed her thoughts about being used, she had allowed herself to feel excited.

'Hi,' she greeted him. 'All ready to go.'

'You look lovely. And again, thanks so much for doing this. It really means a lot. Have you got the ring I gave you?'

'Well, yes. But it's only an engagement ring, you realise.'

'I've also got a wedding ring for you. Here, put it on. Get used to being a married woman.' She slipped on the wedding ring he gave her and put the engagement ring on top. 'There you are. Welcome to Mrs Thomas.' She gulped. It felt nice to be loved, she thought, and felt almost teary at the thought of what was to come. She swallowed hard and smiled at the man she loved.

'Okay. I'm good to go. I have a case to put in the back.'

'Fine. There's plenty of room.' He lifted her case into the car and she went to lock up the door. 'Just a minute,' he said, following her. He pushed her inside and shut the door. 'We can't go off without a decent welcome.' He kissed her very thoroughly and she began to feel quite weak.

'I think we should go before I decide I can't go at all,' she managed to whisper.

'We could be a little late. I'd like to take you to bed right now, actually.'

'It does sound very appealing. But I think we should save ourselves for later.'

'If you insist.' She giggled and told him it was sensible. 'Since when were you sensible?' he murmured, still kissing her between his words.

'Come on. Let's get off to London. There are so many things I'd like to do.'

'Spoil sport. Okay, we'll hit the road now. I do need to talk to you about the wedding we never had. Just so we're agreed in case we're questioned in some way.' They finally left Barstow and set off along the motorway. Being a Friday, it was fairly heavy traffic and they sat in queues for some of the journey.

'So, what was our wedding day like?' she suggested.

'Snowy?'

'Nah. That would limit what I could have worn. It was last June. August.'

'Make up your mind.'

'September, maybe.'

'Okay. Last September. That will explain why it's still so new. We live in your house. Where did we meet?'

'Why not be as truthful as we can be.

Say we met at college and got friendly over coffee.'

'Okay. We used to stop over at the coffee bar and get pissed. For how long?'

'I don't know. Six months?'

'Six months of coffee? That would do some damage to our insides.' They both laughed.

'We started to go out together seriously after a month of coffee. I could cope with that.'

'Then we decided to marry and did so in September.'

'But we'd have been starting back to college in September. Better make it in August?'

'Okay. We married on August the fifth.'

'That was a Sunday. I know it was because it's my parents' anniversary and we had a lunch party to celebrate. Besides, that's too early in the month.'

'Okay. Twenty-fifth.'

'And where was the ceremony?'

'In Barstow. Not in the church. I

never fancied a church wedding.'

'Okay. Registry office. Just a very small affair. Just our parents and a couple of friends. I wore a blue outfit. Dress and jacket. I carried a single pink rose. I put it on my grandmother's grave following the ceremony.'

'Now you're getting maudlin. At last, we're moving again. That's a relief.'

They found their hotel remarkably easily. They signed in and were shown to their room. It was lovely. A large bed dominated the room and he bounced on it to test it.

'Nice,' he said. 'Why don't you come and try it?' She did so.

'What do you want to do this evening?' he asked her, some time later.

'I don't really know. Some dinner, of course. You wouldn't last five minutes without a proper meal. Then go on somewhere? I'm not sure where exactly.'

'I won't suggest a club. I don't see you as a club sort of person.'

'You're right there. But if you wanted to?'

'Not particularly. We could just walk around for a bit. Have an earlyish night?'

'Sounds okay to me. Can we walk somewhere? Look in shop windows?'

'You're really quite a romantic aren't you? Okay, we'll do as you suggest. We should eat here though as it's all paid for by the company.'

'You need to tell me what you can about the company. I'd be interested to find out about it wouldn't I?'

He told her about the company. She was most interested to discover it was involved with making parts for aeroplanes, not exactly the planes themselves but with fitting out interiors. It fitted rather well with their own company, and she could immediately see why he'd been called for interview.

'So, as you can see, it would fit my background really rather well. I'm still not quite sure why they wanted to see my wife. But it was almost a condition of entry.'

'Especially when she is a computer genius and could probably save them millions each year if she was also to get involved.' He looked at her, slightly startled by her words.

'So, the difference would be?'

'Nothing at all. I'm just messing around with you. Will I be interviewed at the same time as you?'

'I'm really not sure. Maybe not as they'll probably take you off somewhere else. I'm sorry, love, to put you through all of this; I didn't really think. They simply asked me to bring my wife. I said yes, and then realised I should have simply said I didn't have one. It was too late after that.'

'So, let me say it again. S'pose they offer you the job? What next?'

'I really don't know. I doubt very much they will anyway. In that case, we've had a couple of nights in a London hotel at their expense.'

Joanne felt quite uncomfortable with

the whole business and almost allowed it to spoil her precious time with Mike. She had never loved anyone before and it was muddling her thinking. Whatever happened, she had to keep it to herself and try to enjoy the whole experience for what it offered.

'Come on then. Let's go and eat,' she said, smiling heartily.

It was a huge dining room and they stood at the entrance gazing at the space. The head waiter came up to them and seated them.

'Your room number, sir?'

'Oh, I can't remember. Do you know what it was darling?'

'Six five hundred.' She always remembered numbers.

'Thank you sir, madam. Can I get you something to drink?'

They ordered and he went away.

'Sorry about that. I was about to grope around for the plastic card. I don't know why I didn't remember the number. Silly of me.'

'It doesn't matter. Look, calm down

a bit. You're getting all worked up before you need to. Cool, calm and collected, that's how you need to be.'

'I'm sorry. You're quite right. I've never actually been for any sort of interview before. Dad had organised the factory to make space for me when I finished school. I was never going to university anyway.'

A waiter arrived with their drinks and a vast menu for each of them.

'Wow, that's quite a selection of things to choose from,' he said. 'Come back in a while, will you?'

'Certainly sir.'

For the next few minutes, they were silent. Reading the menu took ages, and at last, she looked at him.

'You must be much more used to seeing menus this size. How on earth do you choose?'

'I suppose I've eaten out a bit more than you. I usually select things dependent on what my companion chooses. But, choose whatever you want. We're not paying, are we?'

'I don't feel comfortable with just eating anything. Okay. I'll have the mushrooms for a starter and then I quite fancy some fish. There seem to be some nice fishy things to choose from.'

When they had finally chosen their food, she asked him where the interviews were taking place.

'Here I think. Some suite they've hired for them.'

'Oh. So any of these other people could be candidates?'

'Maybe so.' They spent the next few minute trying to identify possible candidates and laughing over their choices.

'What about him over there. The elderly man with a bimbo?' she suggested.

'Nah. He's much too young. Or she is, rather. I suspect those two over the other side might be? Red dress for her. Suit for him?'

'Maybe. How many others are there anyway?'

'I have simply no idea. Six or seven couples?'

'Maybe so. That was a wonderful meal. Can we go out now?'

'Fine by me. I love that chocolate pudding by the way. We must try to recreate it somehow.'

'You can. I doubt I could,' she replied with a laugh.

Hand in hand, they walked along past the larger stores. She looked in the windows and gasped at some of the prices.

'Wow, I can really see why jobs in London pay more than where we live. I'd need to work for months if I shopped here.'

'Well, you wanted to see them, didn't you? Be satisfied with what you've got already,' he teased her.

'Oh, I am indeed. I'm very happy with Barstow.' She realised she really was, especially since Mike had come into her life. She squeezed his hand and he smiled at her once more. 'And I'm very happy since I met you,' she added.

'Me too.' He spoke clearly and she felt very pleased with her life. She didn't see the sudden look that crossed his face. He looked very concerned and upset. 'Seen enough for now?' he asked.

'Yes. I'm more than ready for bed now. I can't believe how tiring enjoying oneself can be.'

'Let's go then.'

They made love again and afterwards, lay back talking about the following day. It seemed that he was to be called for his interview after breakfast, at around ten o'clock. She was to be around for some other activity.

'What on earth do you think that might be?' she asked, feeling rather concerned.

'I'm not sure. Maybe they'll organise something. A shopping trip or something maybe?'

'Can't think why. Oh heavens, we'll just have to wait and see. Sleep well and don't worry. We'll show them, won't we?'

Neither of them slept very well. It was all a matter of not knowing what was going to happen.

'Are you awake?' he whispered to her in the middle of the night.

'I'm afraid so.'

'I hope you're not worrying about tomorrow. Today.'

'A bit. I think it's just being in a strange bed. With you there beside me.'

'I know what you mean.' He reached over to her and ran his hands over her body again.

'Is this what old married people really do?' she asked him.

'I've no idea. But we're hardly an old married couple are we?'

'Indeed not. I'm not sure it's a good idea though. I'm not saying I don't like it but you need to be rested for this interview.'

'You're right. I'll try to resist having you so close to me.' He turned over and they both lay there, wide awake but pretending to be asleep.

The next morning, they both dressed

in their smart clothes and went down to breakfast. They were ushered to a large table in another room, where they met some of the other candidates and the organisers of the event. They were introduced to the others and were all cautious in what they said. It was a good job Joanne was there as everyone seemed to have partners.

'Okay, everyone. Listen up. The plans are that the ladies are invited to meet in the hotel lobby after breakfast. They will be taken to one of the art galleries for the morning. Gentlemen, please will you stay around. We're going to interview you one at a time, but will let you know in a while the order in which you're needed. We have a programme later on for you both to join together. Ladies and gentlemen, thank you.' The woman was one hundred percent American with all the suave, sleek appearance of a top executive. She was the organiser of the whole thing and nobody said anything to follow her words. 'Oh yes, our executives will be here in a few moments to greet you all.'

There were murmurs of thanks from the group. They sat waiting for the next thing to happen. Mike gripped Joanne's hand beneath the table.

'You okay, darling?' he whispered to her.

'I think so. Are you?'

'Think so. All a bit strange, isn't it?' he said.

'Very. I'm not sure why we're off to an art gallery. But there it is. I'll try to enjoy it and make sure I ask the right questions.'

'You'll be fine. Finer than I will, anyway. Okay, this looks like it could be the executives.'

Two men arrived, looking very smart and carrying brief cases. They greeted everyone and sat down near the head of the table. After a few moments, one stood up and introduced himself as the Head Honcho of the HR department. No more explanations but he was indeed the Head Honcho, whatever that meant.

'Okay, now we'll be seeing each of you for a half-hour discussion and then a group interview. We'll see the rest of you together with your wives later in the day. Enjoy.'

The females were ushered out and told to meet in the foyer in half an hour. When they were all assembled, awaiting the female organiser (as they thought of her), they stood together. For Joanne, it was a completely new experience. There were three other women, all smartly turned out and all determined to impress. She was not going to say anything to begin with but gave her name when she was asked for it. They were sent out to a large taxi which took them and the organiser, whose name was Cindy, across London to the National Gallery.

'Now I'd love to show you the exhibition on the first floor. We'll try to stay together in a group so we can talk about the paintings. Everyone all right with that?'

They all murmured their assent and walked upstairs to the first floor. Everyone was being very cautious about what they said to each other. One of the others seemed to stick to Joanne and she confided that this was all a bit of a mystery to her.

'My name is Melissa by the way. You are Joanne, aren't you?'

'That's right. What do you do Melissa?' she asked in a friendly way.

'Me? I look after my husband. Entertaining is a large part of our lives. No time for anything else. Do you do something then?'

'I'm a lecturer, actually.'

'Oh my goodness. How do you cope with everything that's needed?'

'We manage,' she said, regretting that she had said anything about her job. One thing she must remember in future. Most of the others were wives first and anything else came second.

'Amazing. I think you must be the only one of us who actually does anything outside their home. Well, apart from lunch clubs and that sort of thing. Oh dear, we now have to speak about these wretched paintings.'

The organiser was speaking about various pictures very knowledgeably. The other wives were hanging onto her every word, nodding madly and agreeing with everything she said. Joanne was already feeling quite fed up with the whole process.

'Interesting what you were saying. I'm not sure I can agree with you,' she said at last. The other three wives stared at her.

'Really? Why not?' the organiser replied.

'I don't actually think they were all painted during the same period. For instance, look at this one. It is quite a different style to, say, the one over there. Same artist but a different agenda. Sorry. Just my opinion.'

'Quite a valid one. What do you think? Melissa?'

'Oh, I agree entirely with what you were saying. Very interesting though.'

She smiled sweetly at the woman, wanting to appear completely at one with her.

'I see. Sophia? What do you think?' The wife called Sophia also agreed with the organiser, as did Susanna. It seemed Joanne was on her own. So what? She wasn't supposed to fit in with everything the American said. This wasn't what it was all about. She wondered how Mike was getting on and sent him a good wish mentally.

The tour continued. Eventually, the organiser decreed it was time to go back to the hotel for lunch. Joanne was delighted. She felt wearied by these somewhat vacuous women and really felt as if she might like to talk to the organiser on her own. She wanted to tell her that she was a busy lady herself and that, as a lecturer, she wasn't living in a world of flower arranging and lunch clubs and housework. Somehow, she didn't feel any of them did a great deal of housework on their own. They probably all had someone who came in daily to clean up their mess. She suddenly longed for her own home and her own mess around her. But she was here as Mike's so-called wife, and live it through she must. She didn't want to ruin his chances, but was horribly afraid she just might say the wrong things.

11

They all arrived back at the hotel and were shown into the suite they had hired for the interviews. Their men were all drinking, mostly water, and chatting freely. The women joined their husbands with a great show of affection.

'How was it all?' Mike asked as quietly as he could.

'Interesting. I loved some of the paintings but I was very much on my own. The trouble is, none of them know anything much about anything.' She spoke softly, so the others couldn't hear what she was saying. 'Anyway, how did your interview go?'

'Rather a strange one actually. They asked me nothing about what I do or what the business is, and just asked me for my thoughts on various things.'

'Hi Joanne,' said Melissa from behind.

'Oh Melissa, meet Mike. This Melissa who is married to Charles, is that right?'

'Sure is. See, I'm getting the hang of this USA stuff aren't I?'

'Oh yes indeedy.'

'We're going to eat. You want to join us?'

'Okay, thanks,' Mike replied. 'You ready to eat, darling?'

'Sure am,' Joanne said with a wink. The four of them went to the buffet and helped themselves to the food. 'This all looks lovely, doesn't it?'

'Not too bad I suppose,' Melissa said. 'I would never put the salmon out quite that way but one can't argue with supposed masters of their trade. How did things go with you this morning, Mike?'

'Not bad, thanks. How did you do, Charles?'

'Quite well, I felt. It's all a bit formal in a way. Formal and informal at the same time. I'm going for some of the beef I think. Do you think that's sensible, darling?' he asked his wife.

'Let's go over there to sit,' Joanne suggested as soon as they were served. 'I can't stand this pussyfooting round. Drives me barmy.'

'We do need to talk to the others though. I need to know what I'm up against.'

'Okay. Whatever. I'll try to remain polite for the rest of the day. Can you manage there, Charles?' She saw him struggling to manage his plate and leaned over to help him.

'Thanks. Thank you very much. Joanne, isn't it?'

'That's right. I'm with Mike, here.' Stupid thing to say. Obviously she was with Mike. That's why she was sitting next to him. They struggled to chat over the meal and she decided she needed the loo. Anything to get away from this wretched couple.

She stood looking at herself in the mirror. She combed her hair and re-applied some make-up.

What on earth was she doing here?

Pretending to be Mike's wife for some poxy job he'd applied for, hating the other people he was in competition with and, by now, feeling positively bored. She sighed and went back to join the group, a smile fixed on her face.

'Okay, is everyone back with us?' the organiser asked. 'We're going to play a few little games now. Could you each pair of you sit together at a table by yourselves? There should be enough space. That's right. Now, here are some sheets with questions for you to answer together.'

Joanne and Mike took their sheets and answered the questions right away. They finished long before the rest and sat looking at each other in amazement. Stupid questions, she thought.

'Okay. Pass them in now.'

'Sorry, we haven't quite finished,' said Sophie.

'No worries,' responded the organiser, handing out more sheets. 'This one is a scenario of a plane crash. Discuss how you'd get the passengers off the plane.'

'What, between the two of us or all together?' asked Mike.

'Between the two of you for five minutes. Then we'll take it as a group thing.'

They read through their paper and chatted about the way they'd take everyone off the plane.

'We did something like this on a training day at college,' Joanne whispered to him.

Five minutes later, the organiser asked each of the four pairs for their thoughts. The others had some good ideas but Joanne and Mike had the best solutions.

'Hooray for our college training days,' she mumbled to him.

'Okay. Thank you very much, ladies and gentlemen. We're going to chat among ourselves and we'll let you know the results of our chats in a little while. Maybe you'd like to go and freshen up or maybe find some tea? I'll see you back in here in half an hour.'

They decided to go to their room for a few minutes' rest. Some of the others went for tea.

'I've nearly had it for today,' she told him. 'I really can't stand much more of Melissa and Charles. How about you?'

'I'm done with all of them actually. What do you want to do this evening?'

'I really don't know. You fancy a show?'

'I'd love to see several things that are on. Why don't we go to see the concierge? They might let us know what tickets are around.'

'Like that idea. Let them do the searching. Come on then.'

Reinvigorated, they went down to the foyer and asked the concierge to see if he could get them seats for anything that evening.

'Certainly, sir. Your choices would be?'

'I'd love to see one of the musical shows, if there's anything available?' Joanne had a soft spot for musicals and wanted to see anything they could.

'I'm happy with that. We'll call back in a while. Now, it's crunch time for the interviews. Come on, love. Let's see what's happening.'

They were the last to arrive in the suite. Everyone else was sitting around muttering quietly to each other. As the two executives came in, there were mutterings and then silence fell.

'Ladies and gentlemen. Thank you all very much for your time today. We have decided to separate the sheep from the goats and allow two couples to leave us now. Thank you so much for spending time with us but I'm afraid this is the end of the road for you. We'll keep your names in our files and contact you again if anything new becomes available. Charles and Melissa. Thank you so much. It's been a pleasure to meet you but you will not be selected on this occasion. Roger and Sophie, nor will you. Again, very many thanks for your attendance and good luck for the future. You are of course very welcome to stay on for the night at our expense.' The two couples left amidst a shaking of hands and goodbyes.

'This leaves us with Mike and Jeremy. Would it be okay if you two stay on tonight and we come back to talk some more tomorrow? I don't know if this will spoil any plans you have?'

'Fine by me,' Mike told him.

'Me too.'

'Okay then, enjoy your evening. We can organise tickets for a show or a club if you'd like to do that.'

'Thank you, sir. That sounds great,' Jeremy told them. 'You want to join us?' he asked Mike and Joanne.

'Well, we're hoping the concierge has managed to get tickets for a show for us. So, thanks for the offer but I think we're already fixed.'

'Okay, well enjoy yourselves. And congratulations by the way.'

'And to you.'

They all went out and Joanne and

Mike went to the concierge to see what he'd been able to do for them. They were thrilled to hear he'd got tickets for one of the top new shows.

'Oh that's terrific,' Joanne told him. 'I hope it wasn't too difficult for you.'

'No, not at all. You can collect them at the desk in the theatre. It begins at seven-thirty but you need to pick the tickets up at seven o'clock. I hope that's convenient for you.'

'Thank you so much.' They gave him a tip and went to their room.

'What shall we do about dinner?' Mike asked. 'Eat something now or wait till later?'

'How about a snack now and something else later?'

'Sounds like a plan. I fancy a burger. How about you?'

'What a low taste you do exhibit,' she told him. 'Okay, a burger it is.'

They both changed and went out to enjoy their evening. It was a great show and they stopped off for something to eat on their way back.

'You've made it to the last pair in this interview. If they offer it to you, what will you do?'

'I'm not actually sure. Still, it's been an interesting experience, don't you think?'

'I suppose so. I've enjoyed the trip to London anyway so thank you for that. But I feel a bit concerned about the next stage in the process.'

'Don't you worry about that. Come on, let's finish up now and then I can take you to bed. I feel on a high now.'

They arrived back at the hotel and went straight to their room.

'I could do with a shower,' Joanne told him. 'I feel all dusty and dirty.'

'I'll join you in there. It's quite large enough.'

'What, at the same time as I'm in there?'

'Why not? It could be different.'

She laughed and stripped off her clothes. He did the same and together they went into the shower. They both stood, allowing the water to pour over them. He asked her to wash his back, which she did, rather slowly and very sensuously. She rather enjoyed the feel of his skin beneath her ministrations. He was becoming more and more ready to take her but he breathed deeply to calm himself. He turned to do the same for her, lingering in the same sort of way, washing her carefully and making her squirm with pleasure. They turned to face each other once more and suddenly, it became so much more intense. He pressed her against the wall and entered her. She groaned and hooked her legs around his waist. He had his arms stretched over her, resting against the shower wall.

'Oh my dearest love,' she murmured, unable to stop herself. He slowed down and eventually stopped his movements. He smiled at her but she couldn't help wondering what she'd done. She said no more. She released herself and reached for the towels, drying him first and then waiting for him to dry her. They fell into bed and he seemed to go to sleep quickly. She lay awake, thinking about her words. Whatever had she said that had affected him so much? It was all so silly. Yes, she knew she loved him more than anyone else she had ever known, but why was he so peculiar about being serious with her? What was he trying to hide from her? At last, she fell asleep, but was woken by him getting out of bed and causing a draught.

'What's up?' she murmured sleepily.

'It's eight o'clock. I thought I should get up and get ready for breakfast. Are you going to wake up, sleepy-head?' He leaned over her and kissed her once more. Everything seemed fine this morning. She stretched and welcomed his attentions.

'We could always skip breakfast,' she suggested.

'Well yes, but I'm not sure that would be a good idea. Come on, you. We have work to do today.'

'You and your work,' she grumbled. 'No rest for anyone around here is there?'

They went down for breakfast and

saw Jeremy and Susanna and felt they really should join with them.

'Ready for the battle?' asked Jeremy.

'I didn't realise it was destined to be a battle,' Mike responded slightly too quickly.

'Only joking, old boy. Survival of the fittest and all that.'

'Did you sleep well?' Joanne asked his wife.

'Not really. It was very warm in our room. I was also a bit concerned about what we are to do today. Aren't you worried?'

'I don't think so. Not at all really. It may be quite a formal interview but I somehow doubt that. If both of us are present, it won't be so bad I'm sure.'

'It's all very well for you. You're used to speaking to people en masse whereas I am not. A dinner party at home is my limit.'

'I suppose that could be some sort of restriction. I'm sure you'll be fine. Jeremy is well up for the job, isn't he?'

'Oh yes. I just don't want to let him down.'

'I'm sure you'll be fine. I'm going to get something cooked now. Anyone else want anything?' She got up and went to the hot food counter. Mike followed her.

'You're doing a good job in calming her nerves,' he commented. 'Well done.'

'Thanks. Perhaps I should be doing the opposite, to better your chances.' She was still slightly upset by his reaction the previous night. She had only said 'my dearest love'. What was wrong with that?

'You carry on doing what you do best,' he instructed her with a smile. Why did he have this effect on her? One smile from him and she was putty in his hands again.

They arrived back at their table carrying loaded plates. Susanna stared.

'How on earth can you eat like that?' she asked.

'Not a problem for me.' Joanne smiled at her and began to eat. They were almost finished when the two Americans arrived in the dining room.

'Ah, there you are. When you're done, come into the suite. All four of you please.'

'Fine. We won't be long,' Jeremy told them. 'Are you not eating?'

'We ate earlier. When you're ready, come on through to join us.'

Joanne and Mike continued to eat while the other two left them. She raised an eyebrow to him and he smiled once more.

'Nobody is going to interrupt my breakfast,' he said calmly. 'We'll do as he said. Go to join them when we're ready. Do you want some more coffee?'

Fifteen minutes later, they went to join the other two candidates.

'There's a new information pack for you over there,' Jeremy told them. 'Stuff about the company. I'm not entirely sure now why they want to recruit from the UK. They seem pretty well set up as far as I can see.'

'Who knows?' Mike replied, sitting down with the pack. He handed part of it to Joanne to look through.

'Interesting,' was her comment. 'It says here they have a large proportion of Brits in their factory. Maybe us Brits have more skills than the US parts of their work force.' The others smiled, obviously very nervous.

The two executives came back to the room and sat down to discuss the plan for the morning.

'We shall need an hour with each couple. We'll see you separately and then have our discussion. We'll see both of you together as a partnership and then you'll be free to go or do whatever you want to do. You'll be notified tomorrow before we fly back home again. Is that clear?'

'That's fine, thanks,' Mike said. Two more half-hour interviews and they'd be ready to leave. He felt confident with Joanne beside him and squeezed her hand to encourage her.

'Okay. I'll start with Jeremy and Susanna and my colleague here will see Mike and Joanne. As this will be the last time you are all together, I'd like to thank you very much for coming along here. Whichever one wins the contract, we'll soon be seeing plenty more of each other.' They all laughed politely and Jeremy and his wife left the room with the one executive.

'Okay guys, now this is all quite relaxed. I want to talk with you about how you see yourself fitting into the role.' His accent was quite strong and Joanne found herself almost laughing at his words. The interviews continued, getting more serious with the questions they were being asked. She felt very proud of the way Mike was dealing with them and was determined she would be a help to his cause. Joanne was asked how she would fit into the new system and how she'd cope with life in the States.

'I expect I'd fit in quite well. I'm pretty flexible in my own work. I'm used to planning my work on my own and fitting into whatever situation it throws at me.'

'And would you wanna work in

USA?' he asked. She looked quickly at Mike.

'Oh yes. I couldn't face being a wife who only went out to lunch. I'd like a job lecturing if I lived there. Or maybe working on computer systems in a company. I don't really mind.'

'Okay. Good answers from both of you. I'd enjoy working with both of you. Maybe we can find something within the organisation for you too, Joanne. I think we're about done here. I'll take you through to next door. You can see my colleague and then you're free.'

'Thanks very much,' said Mike as they shook hands.

'Hope I haven't spoilt your chances,' she muttered as they went to the next room.

'Course not. You were brilliant. I could almost see you catching the next flight out there.'

'Don't you believe it,' she said quickly. 'I'd need to think hard about it all.'

The second part of the interview was much more onerous. Mike answered his questions well and she supported him in some places. At last, it was all over. They left the suite and went back to their room.

'Phew. That was exhausting,' Mike commented.

'You are not kidding. I doubt Charles and Melissa would have coped as well as you did,' she said with a smile.

'What do you want to do now? Eat here or pack up and go home?'

'How about packing up and loading the car? Then we could eat.'

'Sounds good to me.'

'First thing I need to do is get rid of this wretched suit. I seem to have been wearing it for days on end. I'm going to change first, before I start packing.' She peeled off her jacket and the neat shirt she was wearing. She removed the skirt and stood there wondering what she was going to wear.

'You're very lovely you know,' he told her. He was sitting on the edge of the bed and watching her undress. She turned round to look at him.

'Thank you. You know, that's the first really nice thing you've said to me this weekend.' She leaned down to kiss him.

'I'm sorry. I really do appreciate everything you've done for me. I'm sure you made a huge difference to my chances.'

'For the job you don't really want?'

'I'm not sure now. They made life in the USA sound really good.'

'I still don't really want to go though. It all seems so different from everything here. I love my life here.'

'Let's see what happens. Come here and give me another kiss.' He patted the bed beside him and she did as she was asked. 'What's the time?'

'Half past eleven.'

He began to kiss her passionately, and soon they were embroiled in making love. She was determined not to spoil anything this time and remained very quiet.

'What is it?' he asked her. 'You're not

usually this quiet.'

'I don't want to spoil anything.'

'How would you do that?'

'I did last night. In the shower.'

He was silent for a few moments.

'I don't want to hurt you. Not in any way. I really can't allow myself to say anything . . . not yet. You did shake me rather when you said I was your dearest love.'

'Oh, don't let that worry you. It was just me being all emotional. I'm right over it all now.'

'That's good. I'd hate to hurt you in any way. I'm just clumsy at times. Are we all right again?' he asked anxiously. She replied by kissing him one more time.

'Come on. We need to get our packing done. Then lunch.'

Sunday lunch at the hotel turned out to be quite an event. The dining room was well filled as people came in from the street to eat there. They thoroughly enjoyed the whole occasion, made especially nice by knowing the American company were paying for it all.

'I feel a bit mean making them pay,' she said. 'I really enjoyed all of that.'

'Don't let it trouble you. They had their money's worth out of us. You were brilliant at the games, as they called them, yesterday. Left me ages behind. I suspect we were the only pair who completed them all.'

'Just something I've always been able to do. And the show last night. That was wonderful, wasn't it? It's one I really wanted to see.'

'It was amazing. Now, are you ready to make our trip back to Barstow?'

'Afraid so. I could really stay on here for ages. Lovely hotel and lovely city.'

'Let's hit the road then.'

They drove back happily enough. Joanne felt they had moved on in their relationship but she still worried about what would happen if he was offered this job. Maybe if he asked her to marry him? But could she bear to lose all her life and friends? Her parents would hate it if she went to

America. Problems, problems.

'I really need to go home now,' Mike told her. 'Is that all right with you?'

'That's fine. I have work to do before tomorrow, anyway.'

'Thank you again for everything. I really do appreciate it.'

'Let me know the outcome, won't you?' she asked.

'Of course. I'll text you tomorrow. In case you're too busy to speak.'

'Okay. I'll look forward to hearing from you.' They kissed each other goodbye and he drove away.

'Damnation,' she said, looking down at her left hand. 'I never gave him the rings back.' She kept them on for the evening, pretending they were real.

'Oh Mike, Mike,' she whispered. 'Why is everything so difficult?'

12

It was barely ten-thirty the next day when Joanne got her first text from Mike.

'I got it!' was what it said. 'Have to reply acceptance within 24 hrs. Help me!'

She texted him back. 'Well done. Are you accepting?'

'Dunno. Can we meet this eve?'

'Okay. Come round when you're ready.'

She could scarcely concentrate for the rest of the day. She had firmly decided she would not go with him. It would be a quick *divorce*, she had decided. But if he asked her to marry him, what would she do then? She tried hard to concentrate and finally managed to get through the day. She arrived home at the same time as Mike.

'I couldn't get on at work anymore,'

he said. 'So I decided to take a timeout. So, what do you think? About the job offer?'

'Congratulations. I'm delighted you got the job. Your next decision is yours alone.' She spoke in a manner that felt rather detached from everything, as if it didn't matter to her.

'Thank you. You do seem somewhat cautious in your response.'

'Well, thinking about it, I really don't think it has a lot to do with me.'

'But you were instrumental in making it all happen. You know that.'

'If it was down to me that you got it, then you were silly to ask me to join you. Oh goodness, Mike. What do you want me to say? You knew the risk you were taking. I came with you because . . . well, because I did.'

'Wouldn't you consider coming with me? Please think about it?'

'Not just as me. I might think about it if . . . well, if we were married. But there's no chance of that happening, is there?'

'I don't know what you want me to say.'

'Then there's no more to be said on the matter. Oh, I've still got your rings. I'll get them for you.'

'There's no hurry. Leave it for now.'

'Very well. Do you want something to eat?'

'That would be nice. Thank you.'

The two were so polite and uncommunicative, it was becoming quite painful. Joanne cooked something for supper and they ate it silently. At last she spoke to him.

'So, what's wrong with me? Why couldn't you want to marry me?'

'Well, I do. But I have a problem. Nobody else in the family knows about it and I really can't tell you about it now. Please don't ask me to explain about it all now. If you really won't consider coming to America with me, then I'll turn the job down.'

'But you're turning down a whole load of money and endless opportunities. You really need to think this through properly.'

'Without you in the deal, I suspect they wouldn't want me anyway. Remember they interviewed us as a pair. It was surely down to the answers you gave that they agreed to employ me, us. He even said they'd probably find you a job in the organisation. I suspect that without you, they wouldn't want me.'

'It's all too much for me to deal with. I suggest you go home now and really give some thought to it all. If you turn it down, then it's your job lost. I don't want to think about it anymore. I'll see you again later in the week when you've made your decision. Whatever your problem is with me, then it's up to you to sort it out.'

'Oh Joanne. Please don't be this way. I really do . . . well, I do love you. But I simply can't marry you. Not for a while yet. I'm so sorry. I will sort it out, I promise you.'

'Let me know when you have, then. And you know I love you. Go home now.'

Sadly, he left her. He kissed her once more and it felt horribly like the end of everything. She washed the dishes and sat in front of her computer, staring into space. She went to bed early and lay awake for much of the night. It was Tuesday tomorrow, she realised. She wondered if Mike would arrive at her class that afternoon. How would he react to his job offer?

When he failed to arrive the following day, she felt as if her world was ending. He'd said he loved her, hadn't he? But . . . there was always a but. Trisha met her on her way out to her car.

'What's up with you? You look so miserable.'

'I think we're all through. Mike and I. It's a bit sad and I just feel a bit depressed about it all.'

'Well come and have supper with us. Not sure what you'll get but it's all on again with us. Was it the woman I saw him with, that night?'

'No. It's a job in America. He's been

offered an excellent post over there and he wants to go. I don't really want to go. I suspect he's agreed to it. Not to worry. Plenty more fish in sea, as they say.' She said it without any enthusiasm.

'Come on round to my place. Follow me home, why don't you?'

'I think not, really. But thanks very much for asking me. I'll be fine. It's okay. He didn't turn up to my class today so that was why I'm a bit down. I'll see you tomorrow.'

'If you're sure. I'll call you later.'

'Don't worry about me. I'm fine. Really.'

She got into her car and drove away, giving Trisha a friendly wave as she passed her. Hopefully, she'd take that as a signal that all was well in the world of Joanne, even if it wasn't.

It was a long week. She heard nothing more from Mike and she assumed he was probably packing for his trip to America. She could plan to go and see her parents at the weekend.

Why had she been so happy before? She had rarely gone to see her parents except when asked to go, and here she was thinking she would go to see them. Now, everything hung heavily around her and she was getting more and more fed up. She was about to call her parents when there was a knock at her door. She went to open it and there stood Mike, a large bouquet in his arms.

'I'm so sorry,' he began. 'I'm sorry to have used you in the way you must have felt you were being used. Here, please take these before I drop them.'

'Come in. And thank you very much. They are lovely. The flowers I mean. I take it this is a farewell gesture?'

'Farewell? No, of course it isn't.'

'So are you going to America or not?'

'I'm not. I haven't actually told my father yet. He still thinks I might be going. I told the company thanks for asking me but I'd decided against. They weren't too pleased.'

'Gosh, I bet they weren't. After all of

that last weekend. Will they offer it to Jeremy?'

'I have no idea. Look, can we go out somewhere this evening? I feel the need to treat you to a meal out at the very least.' She was surprised. But he'd turned down the job so that must mean something. Were things going to be okay again?

'I suppose going out is an option. I haven't cooked anything yet. Give me time to put these in water and to change.'

'Excellent. Oh, and I'm sorry for not turning up at your class this week.' She waited for his excuse but none came. She shrugged and left the room.

He sat down and looked at a magazine that was lying around. He so much wanted to go upstairs and watch her change but he knew it was the wrong thing to do. How could he possibly explain about his problems to her? He was saving up every penny he earned and once he'd been able to sort out his problems, he would make it up to her. Meantime, he had a huge favour to ask of her.

'You look nice,' he told her; though she was wearing one of her hippy-style skirts which he liked, but knew that it didn't do her justice.

'Sorry, I haven't got very much to choose from in my wardrobe. It's seriously due a makeover.'

'Where do you want to go to?'

'Up to you. I'm happy with whatever you fancy. Burgers or no.'

'McDonalds it is then.' She caught his grin as she got into his car. She knew he had somewhere special in mind.

They went to a lovely little pub near the river. It had a cosy dining room and was full of people. He had reserved a table, high in the hopes that she would accompany him. He was planning to telephone to cancel if by chance she refused to go with him.

'This is very pleasant,' she told him. 'Well done for securing a table. There aren't any other spaces at all.'

The waiter took their order for drinks and came back with them, bearing a menu for each of them. They chose their dishes while they were drinking. He wanted a steak and she once again chose fish. She felt very comfortable with the evening. Perhaps everything was going to be all right after all. They weren't about to finish, though marriage didn't seem to be on the cards. Was she happy about that? Maybe.

'I have a huge favour to ask you.' She paused in her eating. Whatever did he want her to do now?

'Go on,' she said.

'You said you'd come to look at our system and make some suggestions. Dad's agreed to it if the offer is still open. We have a problem in reconciling various parts of it in the deal, and it needs a bit of something doing to tweak it.'

'Is that all? I was expecting something far more sinister than that. Okay, I'll come round and take a look. How was he about the job?'

'He was slightly disinterested as a matter of fact. He still thinks I'm probably going to America, as I said.'

'Oh you are wicked,' she laughed. 'Keeping the poor man hanging by a thread like that.'

'He's amazingly amenable to my suggestions at present. It's worth it to keep him on-side. He's listened to a whole heap of suggestions lately.'

'That's all good isn't it?'

'Well yes, I suppose it is. I suspect he wants everything sorted before I leave. I'm very much in charge of everything computer-oriented. He is in charge of the machinery that makes things and I do the computer stuff. Except I can't make something work.'

'I'll come and take a look at it. Course I will.'

'That's very good of you. Thanks a lot.'

'Here comes our food. It looks wonderful. Much better than anything I'd have cooked at home.' They both tucked in and were silent for a while.

'Oh yes, there's a family wedding coming up soon. Will you be my plus one?'

'Who's getting married?'

'Some cousin. We're not close but Mum seems to think I should go. I'd be very pleased if you came with me. As yourself and not being engaged or anything. No strings, I promise you.'

'Now there's a breakthrough,' she replied. 'Okay. When is it?'

'A week tomorrow.'

'Heavens. I'd better find something new to wear. I'll go shopping before then. How posh is it?'

'Fairly posh, I expect.'

They chatted comfortably for the rest of the evening, nothing too demanding waiting round the corner, she hoped. But she had come to realise that with Mike, one could never tell what lay round the corner. She felt certain she could sort out their computer problems quite easily. By the time they returned home, she was uncertain of what he expected. She invited him in and he was delighted.

'How's the upset with your flatmate?' she asked him.

'Still ongoing I'm afraid. I feel I'm on the way out of that place in the near future.'

'What will you do?'

'Go back home I suppose. It will mean a pause in my escorting duties, although with you in my life, I can always use you as my excuse, can't I?'

'Oh yes of course. I'm always around to be an excuse for something.'

'Sorry, that wasn't meant to sound that way.'

'I am a little weary of being your excuse for everything in sight.'

'I'm so sorry. I really didn't mean it to sound like that. Oh heavens, I've put my foot in it again haven't I?'

'You have indeed. But never mind. When shall I come round to look at your system?'

'When are you free?'

'I could come tomorrow morning, if that's any help.'

'That would be terrific. Thanks so much. Now, come here. I've been waiting all night to kiss you.' He did and, some time later, they went upstairs to bed.

The following morning they awoke late. Mike went downstairs to make coffee and brought it back to bed.

'I wasn't sure about toast. Shall I go and make some?'

'Let's drink the coffee first and then decide. Big decisions like that need time.' They snuggled down again after drinking their coffee and she was close to falling back to sleep.

'Hey, sleepy-head. We need to go to the factory this morning. And you have shopping to do today. You need to wake up.'

'Bully,' she murmured, pretending to be sleepier than she really was.

'I'll go and make some toast,' he said, nearly managing to slip out of the bed. She grabbed him and held him down. She laid him on his back and sat on top of him.

'I'm going to teach you a lesson for always thinking you can rely on me,' she told him. She felt quite brave today and was going to take the initiative.

'I did say I was sorry, didn't I?' he protested somewhat feebly, loving what she was doing to him. He relaxed, allowing her leeway to do whatever she wanted.

'You did, but then you did it again. Put on me. Assumed I'd be willing to take the blame for whatever you were doing.' All the time she was speaking, she was exciting him till he felt so weak he felt as if he was about to come. 'Stop doing that,' she ordered him. 'You can just wait for me.' She laid over him and held him there, waiting for her permission. He groaned, wanting her so much it almost hurt. At last, she allowed him inside her and together, they reached their climax. She lay on top of him for several minutes and they gradually came down from their high. She grinned at him. 'Now you can go and make me some toast.'

By the time they reached the factory, it was getting close to lunchtime. He powered up the machine and she looked at the various components. She took some time looking before she attempted to work on it.

'Shall I go and get us a sandwich or something?' he asked her.

'Sounds like a plan,' she muttered, totally lost in her thoughts.

He went away and drove out to the snack shop nearby. She was oblivious to him having left her there. She ate the sandwich he'd brought but was totally engrossed in her work, not speaking to him much. At about three o'clock, she came back to life.

'Okay. I suspect the problem is with the software. I've written a small program to get round this but I think you need an upgrade and very soon. I know this will be expensive but it is very necessary.'

'I doubt the old man will accommodate it. He is so pessimistic about getting value from anything. Anyway, I will tell him. And thank you so much for all your efforts. You've been brilliant at doing it.'

'I'm pleased to help. If you do get the new program, I'll come and install it for you. Get you running smoothly again. What time is it? If I'm to go shopping, I need to move, I should think.'

'I'll take you into town and drop you off while I find a parking space. There isn't much time before the dress shops all close. You could be lucky and find the perfect item right away.'

'You obviously haven't been shopping lately,' she commented.

The following week was a busy one for her. Between her lectures, she made several sorties into the shops, but by Friday she had found nothing suitable to wear to a posh wedding. She would have to call it off. Mike was not going to be too pleased but it was the only solution. She phoned him on the Friday evening.

'I'm so sorry but I really can't come

with you tomorrow. I can't find anything suitable to wear.'

'Don't be silly. Of course you must come. You must have something in your wardrobe that will do. I'll be round later to help you look.'

'There really is nothing in there.'

'I'll be round after work. And I'll bring something to eat. I'll be on my bike. Mel wants the car this weekend. After using it so much recently, I can't say no. Would you be willing to use yours tomorrow?'

'You can borrow it. I really won't be able to come with you.'

'I'll see you later.' He put the phone down. Joanne gave a shrug.

He arrived around six-thirty with a 'meal deal' from a local store.

'Maybe not exactly what you were expecting but I hope it will do. Let's put it in the oven and see exactly why you think you can't come with me.'

At the back of her rail of clothes were an elderly dress and jacket she hadn't worn in ages. He dragged them out and suggested they were perfect.

'But they're ancient,' she told him.

'I haven't seen them before and nor will anyone else there. Problem solved. Now, let's go and eat.'

She gave a sigh and went downstairs again. If he thought it would do, who was she to complain?

The following day was bright with winter sunshine. Mike had gone round to his flat to get ready and returned some time later, still using his bicycle. She smiled at him in his best suit and cycle clips. She too was all ready, changed into what she saw as her old dress and jacket.

'I really feel a bit jaded in this old thing.'

'I can't see why. It looks lovely. So, are you ready?'

'All ready to go. I'll get the car out.'

It was a pleasant service with a pretty bride and the groom suitably nervous. They took photographs outside the church and were on the verge of leaving when there was a new arrival. Mike blanched and looked as if he were about to pass out completely.

'Sarah?' he said softly.

'Hallo my darling. I thought I'd surprise you.'

13

Joanne froze as this girl came to Mike and kissed him with all the passion she might have shown him herself.

'How are you, my love?'

'F . . . fine.'

'It's wonderful to see you again. I managed to get a flight at the last minute, and now I'm home for ages. Plenty of time for us to get married.'

'I'll wait for you in the car,' Joanne managed to mumble.

'Don't you worry about him. I've hired a car. I can take him to the reception.' She flung her words into the air somewhere in Joanne's direction.

'Oh, I see. Mike?'

'It's all right. I'm coming with you. I'll see you later, Sarah.'

'But I can't bear to let you go quite so soon. Who is this woman anyway?' The latter phrase said in a loud stage whisper.

'I'm sorry. This is Joanne. Joanne Swithenbank. Joanne, please meet Sarah. She's an old acquaintance of mine.'

'An old . . . what did you call me? Come on now, darling. I'm your fiancée. Or had you forgotten about me?'

'Not at all. How come you decided to come back over here?'

'Three months' leave. We'll have time to get married and you can come back with me for a spell after that. A sort of honeymoon.'

'We obviously need to talk. I'll see you at the reception.' He turned away from the girl, took Joanne's hand and walked back to her car. Sarah stood behind them, calling out the sort of comments which should not be heard at anyone's wedding.

'I'm so sorry about what she said. I have to admit, it was a complete shock to see her there. She knew my cousin years ago and I suppose she got an invite.'

'I feel totally shocked, Mike. I really don't think I can face up to meeting everyone at the reception. I'll drop you off and go back home.'

'Please don't. Help me to face her. I really need to explain things to you too. Give me a chance, please.'

'You can come round to see me when you have time. I'm not sure a wedding reception is quite the right place to have this sort of discussion. Now, where exactly are we going?'

'Turn left in about half a mile.' They continued to drive along the road and when they reached the hotel, she stopped outside.

'Go on. Go into the place. I'll see you sometime.' She wanted to get away from it all as quickly as possible. Go somewhere she could disappear. Get right away from Michael Thomas. How could he have a fiancée? How could he? How could he even see her the way he had done with a fiancée in tow?

'Please, Jo. Please come with me.' He

was begging her with every ounce of his ability.

'I can't. Don't ask me again. I really can't come in there with you and that woman. If you ever do sort things out, then you might come and see me again. Goodbye now.'

He got out of the car and she drove away with a flurry of gravel flying up behind her. Her eyes were full of tears. She felt an emotional wreck. Of all things, Sarah whatever-her-name-was was the very last thing she'd expected.

She went home and took off her dress and jacket and flung them down in the corner of her room. She tugged on an old pair of jeans and sweater and thought about the recent weeks in her life. Until she had met Mike, everything had been simple, straight forward and well organised. Now, she had been left emotionally bereft. How many weeks was it since he'd impacted on her? Four, five, six? Whatever it was, she almost wished she'd never even met him. Life was so much easier before he arrived on the scene. No heartache. No emotional turmoil. Men? Forget them. Life was easier without them.

She got back into the car and drove out to the country. She parked and went for a walk in some nearby woods. It smelt cool and damp in there and she walked briskly so as not to get cold. After nearly two hours, she felt hungry. It was already latish into the afternoon. She went to town and bought fish and chips and took them home. One thing about her, she always felt hungry and emotions rarely stopped her from eating. She thought about the disastrous wedding. What on earth was happening there? She pushed the thought away and sat down to eat her fish and chips. Whatever was going on, she felt separated from it all and wanted to keep it that way. She put on her television and tried hard to get involved in whatever was on. She failed miserably.

It was eight o'clock by the time Mike

arrived on her doorstep.

'I don't want to talk to you,' she announced.

'But you must let me explain. Please. Let me in, Joanne.'

'I really don't want to listen to you right now.'

'Please,' he begged. She opened the door wide enough to let him in. 'Let me explain about Sarah. She is the main reason I've been working as an escort. I've been saving up to go and visit her. In a mad moment about a year ago, she merely talked about getting engaged. I wrote to tell her it was the biggest mistake I ever made. I got no reply. I wrote again and still got no reply. I decided that I was going to have to go and visit her. She's been working for a charity in Africa so I was saving up to make the trip. I wanted to tell her that we made a mistake. I mean to say, who gets engaged, goes off to somewhere stupid like that and never even contacts her fiancé?'

'She seems to think she's engaged to

you. She feels she's got a claim on you.'

'Well, she really hasn't. It was all a couple of years ago that we got together and she's now been away for almost a whole year. She hasn't got a ring or anything.'

'I'm sorry but if you ever get free of her, then it will be a different matter. For now, I'd like you to go. Thank you for explaining what you feel is the correct situation as you see it. I'd like to get my life in order once more. Back to the peaceful life I used to lead.'

'But Joanne, you can't . . . '

'Please, leave me now. I need some space.' She rose again and showed him the door. He left her and she immediately collapsed again. She cried for the rest of the evening, despite telling herself that she was well out of it. She went up to her bed and lay on it, fully clothed. She must have fallen asleep in the small hours and finally woke the next day feeling like rubbish. What on earth was wrong with her? When she thought she'd finally found someone nice, it turned out he was a rat bag. She picked up the discarded dress and jacket and dumped it in the dustbin. It felt good.

She set about cleaning the house. She scrubbed and polished and even washed the windows. The phone rang several times, as did her mobile. She ignored both of them. Each time she felt like crying again, she made herself do something else. By evening she was exhausted. She made herself some supper and sat to eat it, watching television. It had reached a silly point when she spent every evening watching television by herself, she thought. She must find other things to do. New things that would get her out and about. What had she done prior to meeting Mike? Watched quite a lot of television, she realised. Far too much television, she realised. She was back at work tomorrow, she thought. She would throw herself into her courses with new heart.

By the time Tuesday arrived, she felt

nervous in case Mike arrived in her class again. She got everything prepared as early as possible and stood awaiting the arrival of her class. Mike arrived along with the others. She smiled at them all and began her lecture. Once they had all settled to their work she wandered round as usual, offering help where necessary.

'I am so sorry, Joanne,' he said to her. 'Please, can we at least have a coffee after the class?'

'Sorry. I have something else to do. Now, is it clear what I asked you to do?'

'I think so.'

'That's good.' She walked away from this man, the man she loved. She had to get over loving him and leave him alone. She really hoped he'd understand and leave her alone too.

'I really need to speak to you in private. Please, won't you have a coffee with me later?' It was the same old story. A coffee after the class and then who could tell what it could mean?

'I'm really busy, I am afraid,' she told

him, her words sounding a little forced. If he knew how much she was shaking inside . . .

'It's just that the software you ordered, or suggested we order, has arrived. My father wants to know if you really are coming to sort it out. Please, won't you come?'

'This is not the time to ask,' she said softly, walking away from him.

The rest of the afternoon was spent looking after everyone else and she left him to work on his own. She felt quite bad about it and later on asked if he was managing his assignment.

'I guess so. Thanks for asking.'

'Look, I'm sorry if I sounded brusque but you know why. I have to get on with my life the only way I know how.'

'I can understand that. I'm just so sorry.' He looked so woebegone that she felt her heart soften. She would speak to him at the end of the class, but it would be on her own terms and she would be the one who was definitely calling the shots.

'Okay everyone. Listen up now please.' When she had all their attention she spoke about her homework assignment. 'Any questions about it?' There were one or two queries which she was able to answer. 'Okay then. I'll see you next week. Leave this week's work on the side before you go please. Thanks everyone. Good work.'

As the group were all leaving, Mike looked at her again.

'Okay. One cup of coffee and you can ask me about whatever it is.'

'Thank you so much,' he said to her. They went across to the students' coffee place and bought their coffee. It was packed solid, as usual. She was briefly tempted to suggest they went to her office but she resisted.

'Sorry, it's pretty noisy here. Tell me what you want to know,' she said.

'It's the new software. I'm struggling to make it work in our system. I wondered if you could help me in some way?' He was practically shouting to make her hear.

'What's wrong with it?' she hollered back.

'I'm sorry. This isn't working for me. I can scarcely hear what you're saying at all.'

'Okay, come over to my office.' She knew it was being silly, stupid, but he really seemed to need to talk about something fairly technical.

She walked across the campus carrying her coffee and staying as far away from him as possible. To give him his due, he didn't try to take any advantage of the situation.

'Okay, now what's the problem?' she asked once they were seated.

'The software you helped with. It's arrived and my father asked me if you were coming over to install it. I might be able to do it but I'd feel much happier if you could come over.'

'I suppose I could come over.' She felt very uncertain about the whole deal and didn't really want to allow herself to be involved again in any way.

'We'd be really grateful if you could.'

'Okay then. When do you want me?'

'As soon as possible really. I know it's difficult for you to fit it in but we really need the system up and running as soon as possible.'

'I have no lectures on Thursday morning. I could come over to you then,' she told him, looking at her diary. 'If all goes well, I can leave you after that to do my afternoon class. I could then come back sometime soon afterwards if there are any problems.'

'That would be terrific. Thank you so much. So, how are you?' he asked tentatively.

'Fine, thanks. And you?'

'I'm in my usual muddle. I have tried hard to clear Sarah out of my life. She does seem to realise that we were never really engaged but I won't be happy till she's gone back to Africa. I don't know how on earth she thought we could be married and she could carry on working there. I suspect she's slightly potty.'

'Well, let's hope it all works out for you. And you're still busily escorting Barstow women around?'

'I've had the occasional call. I'm not really doing much on that front at present.'

'Jolly good. I'll see you on Thursday.'

'Joanne. Please . . . '

'If there's nothing else? Good. I'll see you on Thursday,' she repeated, determined he wasn't going to get any closer to her. He gave a shrug and got up to leave.

'I do love you, you know.'

'Goodbye, Mike.' He turned to leave and she sighed very heavily as he closed her door. What was to stop them now? She had got everything she wanted . . . he had said he loved her and that the wretched Sarah woman was moving back to wherever she came from. Was that enough for her? She'd had a very boring life recently . . . well, for the past week at least. But surely love meant something so much more? The past week had seemed to hang really heavily on her and she knew it was partly her own fault. She had turned down Trisha's invitation to supper on several occasions and steadfastly refused to discuss her affairs with anyone. She would go to Mike's factory on Thursday and do the work his father had asked her to do. What the future brought was up to her as well as him.

By the time Thursday arrived she had worked herself into quite a state. She was up early and got herself ready to move straight from the factory to college in time for her afternoon class. Fortunately, the bosses never minded if their lecturers weren't on site all the time. She drove to the factory, not entirely sure what they knew about the situation between her and Mike.

'Hallo my dear,' Mr Thomas greeted her happily. 'Very good of you to come and see to this computer stuff for us.'

'Hallo. It's not a problem. Or at least I hope it won't be a problem. I'll go through to the office if that's all right? Make a start on the installation.'

'Mike tells me it's going to save money eventually. I just hope he's right. I simply don't understand these things at all. Go on through. Mike's in there.'

'Thanks. Nice to see you again,' she said politely.

'Lovely to see you too. We must fix up for you to come over to have a meal with us very soon.' She smiled and nodded as she went into the office. How very difficult.

'Morning, Mike,' she said. He was sitting at the computer, trying to make something work.

'Good morning. Thanks again for coming over. The software's here. All ready for you to work your magic with it.'

'You can leave me with it,' she told him. In truth, it was always easier if someone left her working on her own.

'Okay. I'll be in the factory if you need anything.' That was good, she thought. No protests or persuasion tactics.

She began her work. It wasn't a simple matter of adding it to the system, but a much more complex task. Things needed moving from one place to the next and she had to keep doing backups. She worked on through most of the morning, interrupted only by cups of coffee. At twelve-thirty, Mike came in once more. Her heart gave its usual leap at the sound of his voice.

'I'm sorry to interrupt you but I felt you should know it's twelve-thirty. I wasn't sure of your plans for the rest of the day.'

'Heavens, is it really? I'm really sorry but it isn't finished yet. I'll have to leave it and come back later on. Is this all right?'

'I'm sure it will be. I won't need to use it for the rest of the day.'

'Okay then. Shove the cover back and I'll be back once I've finished at college. I should be clear by five so I'll see you after that. It isn't such a long job but it's making sure it all works properly.'

'Thanks so much. You must send us a bill in for your expertise.'

'Don't worry about it. I'll see you later.'

She drove away, feeling pleased with both her efforts and the fact that Mike hadn't said anything more about *them*. Maybe they could continue to see each other on a casual basis? She doubted that very much.

14

Joanne's class that afternoon was not her best. She was concerned about the work she had done so far at the factory and was worried that someone might go and try to use the computer. She was also worried that she may not be able to finish it that evening. Besides all of this, she was hungry. It was never a good move to miss lunch but she had done and she was now irritable. Whatever happened after her class, she needed something to keep her going.

As soon as she was finished, slightly earlier than usual, she dashed across to the canteen. She picked up a sandwich pack and a drink and went to her car. She was so hungry that she ate it sitting in the car park. She drove over to the factory and went into the office to settle back to her tasks. Mike was working on one of the machines and waved as she went past. Mr Thomas greeted her and wished her well. He hesitated but left her to it. She worked solidly for an hour before Mike came in.

'Sorry to interrupt,' he apologised, 'but Dad's organised a meal for us at his place. Is this all right with you or too embarrassing?'

'I have to run through a test sequence and then I'll see. I'm not sure.'

'He phoned Mum to get it all set up. I hope you won't find it too much to handle.'

'They think we're still together, I take it?'

'I'm not sure, but it's his way of rewarding you for all your work today. I'll leave you to it.'

She ran the sequence through and everything seemed fine. It was approaching eight o'clock. Could she, would she, go with him to his parents' house? It would seem rude not to.

'I'm through here. I'll just point out the main features and we're done.'

'I'll need to phone home. Will you come or not?' She thought for a moment.

'Okay, but it mustn't be a late one. Now, this here is the main change.' She talked him through it and then they left the factory. She was driving him as he had his bicycle with him. 'How are things with Mel and his girlfriend?' she asked as they drove the short journey.

'Dire in the extreme,' he replied. 'He wants me to move out so they can have their own love nest there. I doubt they'll afford the rent for too long, but I'm staying there till things are sorted with . . . never mind.' He was about to say 'us', she realised.

'I'm sorry to hear that.'

They drove to his parents' home and enjoyed a lovely meal. Joanne felt so hungry she really made the most of it. She was slightly floored when Mrs Thomas asked her when they planned to be married.

'Oh but I don't . . . I mean . . . '

'We haven't even thought of it yet,

Mum.' Mike spoke quickly, seeing Joanne was floundering somewhat.

'Now isn't that a pity?' she replied. 'I'm so looking forward to helping with all the planning.'

'Don't be too anxious, Mrs Thomas. I don't think it will be happening any time soon.' It was the best she could offer in the circumstances. 'And I hope you don't think me too rude, but I really need to leave you now. I have an early start tomorrow and I haven't been home since I left first thing this morning.'

'No of course not. We quite understand.' She winked at her as she left the table. Joanne hated that she still thought the pair were 'engaged'.

They drove back to the factory almost in silence. She really didn't know what to say. As they reached the factory, he broke the silence.

'Thank you so much for coming with me tonight. I really appreciated it and I'm sorry about Mum.'

'I wondered why you hadn't told her

we weren't engaged, but I expect you had some sort of weird idea that if you didn't mention it we could be all on again.'

'Not at all. I haven't mentioned it because that was the first time we'd all been together again. I've been avoiding them really. What with all the arguments about the new software and, well, the business in general, it never seemed worthwhile going over there.'

'How long is this going on?'

'I really don't know.'

'Well, I hope you get it sorted before too long. I'll say bye now. If there are any problems, give me a call.'

'Thanks again. Bye.'

She drove away, her emotions once more jangling together. They hadn't mentioned Sarah or her dramatic appearance out of the blue. Had he managed to get rid of her finally or was she still hovering in the background somewhere? She fell into bed when she arrived home and fell asleep very quickly.

During her lecture the following morning, she received a text from Mike.

'Having dreadful problem with system. Can you call me when you're free?'

As soon as her class was over, she called him.

'What's the problem?' she asked.

'I'm not sure. Each time I try to type in instructions, it all goes a bit haywire. Can you come over later?'

'Okay. I'll come this afternoon. It was all working last night. I can't think what it is. I'll see you later.'

Damn it, she thought. She seemed unable to get away from them. This would be her last visit, she promised herself. They'd have to manage on their own after this. She finished her work and tidied her desk and drove out to the factory once more. It was fortunate that it wasn't too far away. She went inside and went straight to the office.

'So, where are you with it all?'

'I've given up on it. I didn't want to make more of a mess of it than I already have. Shall I leave you to it?'

'Probably the best thing. I prefer to work on my own.' He left her and went into the workshop. She sat down to look at the problems and worked steadily for a while. She heard the doors open and close and then raised voices. She looked round but couldn't see what was going on.

'Mike, baby,' she heard. 'Why are you being so nasty to me?'

'I'm not. Look, we're over. Not that there was anything to start with. It was all in your imagination.'

'Come on now. That just isn't true. We're engaged. You know we are. Okay, so I don't have a ring but that's just timing. We can go and buy one tomorrow.'

'Oh for goodness sake. I don't love you. In fact, truth to tell, I don't even like you. Now please, leave me alone and go and sort out your own problems.'

'Is your father around? I need to talk to him.'

'I'm afraid he's had to go out. What do you want with him? If you think he's going to change my mind about you, you're quite wrong.'

'No. I need to see him on business.'

'I'm not sure what business you have with him, but you'd better tell me what it is. I can pass on your message to him.' Everything seemed silent for a while. Joanne heard nothing for a few moments and looked out to the workshop. The pair were standing very close together near to one of the machines. She felt sick. Why was she hearing Mike protesting so blatantly? He seemed to be in some sort of clinch with the wretched girl. She looked away and worked some more.

'Look,' she overheard once more. 'I really need to organise some more funding. This is partly why I came over. I hoped to persuade your father to send me back with a load of dosh. This place must be doing really well so I'm sure you can spare a few thousand.'

'You'll be lucky,' he scoffed. 'If we

had a few thousand spare, you wouldn't get them.'

'But it's such a good cause. So worthwhile. If you could see the poor little faces of the people over there.'

'Look, I'm sure you're absolutely correct. It's just that we're having dreadful problems ourselves at present. We are nearly going out of business. This is why Dad's gone out this afternoon. He's negotiating a loan from the bank. If he isn't successful this time, we're all out of work. We've just invested in some new software and if J . . . ' He stopped suddenly, realising that Joanne was in the office, probably listening to all of this. 'I'm sorry. You have to go now.' He hustled her out of the room and out of the building. What was going on? Joanne didn't know. Nor did she want to. She had heard enough, and seen enough too. She wanted to get away from all of this as soon as possible. Away from Mike and his family. She would go and see her parents on Sunday, whether they wanted to see her or not. Mike came back into the factory and into the office to speak to her.

'I'm so sorry you had to hear all of that,' he began.

'Not to worry. I'm sorry you're in such difficult times with the business. Don't worry about paying me for my work. Sounds as if you need to preserve every penny.'

'It isn't quite as desperate as it sounded. I made it sound worse to get Sarah off my back. What a pain she is, really.'

'You didn't look as if she's a pain,' she remarked. Mike looked at her sharply.

'What do you mean by that?'

'Nothing. Forget I said anything. Now, this thing seems to be working properly again. I'm not sure what you did but I'll go through it once more and then I must go.' She showed him the various points and he seemed to grasp what she told him.

'But I'm still uncertain about what I did.'

'I think you mixed up the two source elements and the whole thing crashed. Anyway, it's okay now. Try to do it yourself.'

He did and everything worked perfectly.

'Thank you so much,' he told her. 'Let me take you out for a meal or something to say thank you.'

'There's no need. Your thanks are enough. I hope things all work out for you.'

He reached for her and took her into his arms and kissed her. She relaxed against him, loving the feeling once more. He smelled so nice, she thought. She was busy kissing him back when the door opened and his father came in.

'Don't mind me,' he said brightly. She drew back from the man she knew she loved and pushed him away.

'I'm just going,' she managed to say. 'It's all working now.'

'I can see that,' he laughed. 'You get off now Mike. I'm sure there are things you can do, rather than hang around here.'

'How did you get on?'

'Okay. They're willing to extend our credit for another week or two. We just need to get a couple of orders in and we'll be well away. I think I'll make a break now and get home.'

'Okay. If you're sure, I'll go too.' He packed up the computer, leaving Joanne standing there. Covers were put on the machinery and he was ready to go.

'Joanne, please, can't we talk?' he said as they were outside. 'I really need to . . .'

'There is nothing more to say. Goodbye Mike. I'll maybe see you around.' She got into her car and drove away. He stood there, looking after her with a look on his face that was all pure longing. She didn't see his look at all as she drove along the country lane towards her home. Her eyes were filled with tears. She kept blinking them away and arrived home, still shaking slightly from his kiss. He had been kissing

Sarah too . . . hadn't he? He was standing pretty close to her and seemed to care what she was saying. He'd taken her outside when he remembered Joanne was sitting at his computer. She was weary with the whole thing. Thinking about everything that had happened within the past few weeks, she knew she had made the right decision. Live without a man. It rang clearly to her. She picked up the phone and rang her mother.

'How lovely,' her mother said. 'Is there something wrong? I mean to say, it usually takes months for us to persuade you to come over.'

'Of course not. I just thought it would be nice to see you. I'll drive over early Sunday morning.'

'Why not come over right away? We're here and you're obviously at a loose end. You can be here for supper time if you get away now. I've made a casserole, so there's plenty. I can easily put in a few extra vegetables.' She thought about it for a few moments and decided yes, she would.

'That's lovely dear. We'll see you before too long. Don't you want to bring that nice Mike with you?'

'Not this time,' she managed to mumble. She was not going to break down. She was not going to speak about him this weekend. It all meant she wouldn't do any washing or shopping. Did it matter? Not at all. She could do everything on Monday night after work. She rushed upstairs and flung some clothes into a bag. She checked everything was left safe and left the house. She completely missed Mike, who was coming along the road, intent on seeing her.

She arrived at her parents' house in time for dinner.

'Come on in. This is so lovely for us. We can have a proper chat about everything and see what's going on in your life. I take it you've had a falling out with Mike?'

So much for not talking about him.

'We did. It was all very nice when we

were together but he's got so many problems to sort out. We're taking a timeout. Oh Mum, it's so difficult isn't it?' They were in the kitchen while the vegetables were cooking.

'I know it seems like the end of the world when you break up with someone. Maybe you haven't broken up completely?'

'Oh Mum, I really don't know. Life was so much easier when I didn't have anyone else in tow; when I was completely on my own with nobody else to worry about.'

'Anyway, talk as much as you like but these veggies are done. I'll serve in here if you don't mind.'

Joanne and her mother went shopping the next morning. Having planned not to talk about anything to do with Mike, she hardly stopped. Her mother was very tolerant and listened without commenting very much.

'Why don't you buy that dress?' she said. 'You said you needed to update your wardrobe. You can wear it this evening.

We're going to take you out for dinner.'

'That's very good of you. Do you think it might suit me?'

'Go and try it on.' She did and immediately loved it and bought it.

'There you are. See, I can buy things every now and then. I wonder if Mike would like it?'

'Look, love, I don't really know what to say to you.' Her mother was not used to talking about anything in great detail. 'I'm happy to listen to you but I really can't comment. I don't really know him. I only met him at Christmas. It was a nice Christmas, wasn't it?'

'Lovely. Best I remember in ages. But then, Mike was here too, wasn't he?'

'Yes dear, he was. Now, do you want to look for anything else or shall we get back home for some lunch?'

'Might as well get back I suppose. I'm sorry, Mum. I won't talk about him anymore. I realise there's nothing more you can add.'

'Right, well let's go then.'

It was quite a pleasant weekend,

under the circumstances. Her parents clearly were worried about her frame of mind but they did their best to distract her. After lunch on Sunday, she packed up and left them.

'Thanks very much,' she called out through her open car window. 'Lovely weekend.' She waved and drove off. What was the saying? *This is the first day of the rest of your life*. It was something she'd never thought about before but now it seemed appropriate to think about it.

Back in her own place, she began to tidy up and did her washing. Every now and then she thought about that phrase and made some determined effort to believe it. She eventually noticed the answering machine flashing and pressed the play button.

'Joanne, please can we talk? There are so many things we need to sort out. I love you. Please call me when you get this message.'

There was a second message.

'Jo, please call me. I really need to see

you and talk about everything.'

A third message said almost the same again. She hesitated. Then she wondered why he hadn't called her mobile. She fished it out of her bag and saw there were a whole string of missed calls. Why on earth hadn't she heard them? The man was clearly desperate to speak to her. She would think about it and call him later. In any case, how did he know she was back? She pressed the play buttons on her mobile and listened to his lovely voice begging her to call him. She felt very weary of everything and though she wanted to call him back, she needed time to think about what to say. She sat down with a paper and pen and began to write her list.

1. He provides me with a companion I really like.
2. He is lovely.
3. He disrupts my nice pleasant life.
4. He says he loves me but then he is having some sort of relationship with Sarah.

5. He needs to sort out his own life before trying to sort mine.
6. He gets on well with my parents.
7.

She stopped at seven. She couldn't think of anything else to write. Was this truly a summary of everything they meant to each other? She thought some more and penned the rest.

7. He makes too many demands on me.
8. I love it when we're in bed together.
9. I love him.

There it was. Number nine was the killer. She loved him. She picked up the phone to dial his number.

15

The phone rang for ages. Joanne was about to leave a message when it was picked up.

'Hallo,' said a male voice.

'Is Mike there please?'

'Sorry. Can I take a message?'

'It's okay. I'll try his mobile.'

'Okay. Thanks.' He put the phone down again.

'Well, thank you Mel,' she muttered. She dialled Mike's mobile and immediately got voicemail. She switched it off, deciding she would call later. Obviously, he'd gone out somewhere and hadn't got his mobile on. She continued her tasks around the house, finally sitting down to watch television at about seven o'clock. She tried his mobile again but still it was left on voicemail. One more try and she would leave him a message. She felt so frustrated when she was ready to talk to him.

She tried again at eight and this time, decided to leave him a message.

'Hallo Mike. It's me, returning your call. I was at my parents' for the weekend. I'm home again now.'

She sat not watching what was showing and kept looking at the phone. He didn't call. At ten-thirty, she gave up and went to bed. Damn the man. She was not going to put herself out over him. There was still nothing from him by the following day. She gave a sigh and went off to college, planning to start her new life from now on. As for Mike, he could perhaps go to America now, free of all encumbrances. She had moved out of his life.

During the morning her mobile rang. She picked it up to look. It was strange number. Probably one of these wretched PPI people who kept ringing her. She ignored it and continued with her class. Over lunchtime it rang again, the same number. She answered it, ready to shout at whoever was calling her.

'Is that Joanne?'

'Yes,' she snapped. 'Who are you?'

'It's Mel. Look, there's been an accident. Mike's in hospital. I think you might need to go there.'

She sat down heavily.

'Is he all right?'

'We're not really sure. Go round there and see him.'

'Okay. Thanks. I'll go round after work.'

'I think if you can get there earlier, it might be a good idea. I tried calling you earlier. The hospital called me first thing this morning. I'd assumed he'd stayed with you overnight but . . . well, clearly not.'

'Okay. I'll see if I can go soon. Thanks for letting me know.' She was panicking. She had a class starting in a few minutes, but Mike needed her. She'd see her class and start them off on something and then leave them, that was the best thing to do. She grabbed her lesson plan and looked to see where they were. Yes, she would set them an assignment and leave them working on it. She rushed to her lecture room and wrote on the board what she wanted them to do. The students rolled in, clearly not in a hurry, and she quickly called them to order.

'I have to leave you for a while this afternoon. Your assignment is on the board. I want you to work on this and hand in your results next week. Clear?'

'S'pose we don't finish it today?' one of them asked.

'Finish it in your own time and bring it in next week. Okay, sorry but I have to dash.' She shot out of the room and ran along the corridor, odd comments from her class resounding after her. She ignored them and ran across to her car. She drove much too fast and reached the hospital, desperately looking for somewhere to park. There was nothing near the main entrance and she drove to one of the auxiliary car parks. She grabbed the ticket and ran to the main entrance.

'I was told to come,' she panted. 'Mike Thomas? Where is he?'

'One moment please.' The receptionist typed the name into her computer and looked up at Joanne. 'Are you family?' she asked.

'Practically.'

'Well are you or not?'

'I'm his fiancée,' she muttered.

'I suppose it will be all right to let you go up. He's in intensive care. First floor, follow the signs to cardiac unit. You'll see intensive care just after that.'

'Oh my god, oh my god,' she muttered to herself as she ran along the maze of corridors and signs. Cardiac unit, intensive care . . . what on earth was wrong with him?' She arrived outside the ward and found Mike's parents sitting there, looking rather glazed.

'What's happened?' she demanded.

'Mike's been involved in an accident. He crashed the car and, well, he's undergoing surgery at present. Come and sit down dear. It's touch and go I'm afraid.' Mike's mother looked positively shell shocked, and even rather frail.

'But how? When?'

'Late last night it seems. He was lying in his car most of the night, slightly off the road behind some trees.'

'Oh no. So what are his injuries?'

'We don't know yet. They're looking at him now. But he was brought here because he was unconscious.'

'Bad business, all of it. I never liked that girl but I never wished her . . . ' Mr Thomas was speaking.

'Hush now, dear. We don't want to . . . '

'What girl?' asked Joanne, her voice calm and slow.

'Oh dear. That girl who bothered us at the wedding. Sarah someone.'

'She was in the car with him?'

'Well, yes. But she was . . . well, she was killed,' Mrs Thomas told her.

Joanne tried to come to terms with the words she was hearing. What on earth was he doing driving around with that woman late on a Sunday evening? She was worried about Mike, of course she was. But if Sarah was with him, who knew what on earth they were doing? She sat for several minutes before she could speak again.

'I'll wait with you to hear what they have to say about Mike's condition but then I have to go.' She was boiling over with fury inside. It was sad she had died, but why on earth was Mike driving her anywhere? She didn't want to face any of this at present.

'As you like, dear.'

'Damned woman. She's an absolute pain. Was a pain.' Mike's father was still stamping around, cursing and grumbling. He was obviously suffering himself and cursing the world around him was his way of dealing with it all. Joanne had to agree with his definition of the woman. She was a pain. It was after almost two hours that a doctor came out of the room to see them.

'Sorry to keep you waiting for so

long. We've established that he's now stable.'

'Oh thank goodness. He's really all right?' his mother asked.

'We think so. The next few hours are critical. He has a broken leg and he's in an artificially induced coma for a while. The head injuries seem to be superficial but this is the way we deal with him for now.'

'Can we see him?' she asked.

'Well, you can come in one at a time. He's right out of it so don't expect too much.'

'Oh, thank you doctor. I'll come right away. Unless you want to go in first?' she asked Joanne.

'No, it's all right. I'll leave him for now and slip away. I'm so glad he's going to be okay though.'

'He'll want to see you very soon. Please come back won't you?'

'I will. I hope he's . . . all right,' she managed to gulp. She left them all standing talking and went back to her car. She sat in the driving seat and found she was crying, sobbing. Poor Mike, she thought. He didn't deserve this. Whatever he'd been doing with Sarah, he didn't deserve to be lying there so badly injured. She started the engine and drove away.

'Have you got your ticket?' the man at car park the entrance asked her. 'Only you need to have paid for it to open the gate.'

'What?' she asked him, still feeling shocked and out of her mind.

'Your parking ticket. You need to pay for it to open the barrier. Move back out of the way a minute. Park over here.' She backed away from the trapper gate and the next car was able to leave. What on earth was she supposed to be doing? 'Have you got a ticket?' repeated the car park attendant.

'Oh, yes. Sorry. It's here.' She handed it to him. He obviously took pity on her and finally took it and put it into the machine.

'Five pounds forty please.' She groped in her bag for some money and handed it over. He fed it into the machine and gave her the ticket back. 'Right. Now you can go. I'm sorry you had such trouble, miss, but perhaps you'll know what to do next time.'

'Sorry. Yes. Thanks a lot.' She backed again and went out of the car park. She needed to pull herself together. What a day. It was far too late to go back to college now. She had done the unforgivable and left her class to work by themselves. No doubt her head of department would have a few words to say tomorrow. Tough, she thought. She'd face him the next day.

It seemed a very long evening. She switched on her computer to do some work but it was hopeless. She cooked some supper but couldn't eat it. All the time her thoughts ran round in circles. Why was he with Sarah? What were they doing? Where were they going? She wondered if Mel might know something? She dialled his number.

'Mel? It's Joanne. I wondered if you

knew where Mike was going last night?'

'Sorry, not at all. He said he needed to go out and drove away. How is he by the way?'

'Not too good. He's in an induced coma and has a broken leg.'

'Oh lordy. It sounds pretty grim then.'

'They seemed to think this was a precautionary measure. He should be brought out of it tomorrow.'

'Give him my best, won't you? You're all right though?'

'A bit shell-shocked, I guess. The girl who was with him, well, it seems she died.'

'Who was that then?'

'Someone called Sarah.'

'What on earth was he doing with her again?'

'I really don't know. I wondered if you knew something but evidently not. I'll call you again when I know more.'

'Thanks for ringing anyway. Bye.'

That wasn't much use, she realised. She sat for a while longer and finally decided she would go to bed. She probably wouldn't sleep but it seemed like a plan. She lay there, remembering the happy times they had lain here together. She hugged his pillow, the one he'd used, trying to capture his smell, his presence. She felt tears burning once more. She would go to the hospital again the following day after work was over. She could be cool and casual about it by then. And she would know how to use the car park and its wretched ticket system. Five pounds and forty pence, she thought suddenly. That was a scandal. She must write to someone to complain.

Joanne arrived at the hospital after college. She had somehow survived her day and had met no problems for leaving her class the previous afternoon. Hopefully they'd worked quietly and nobody had noticed her absence. She went into the main entrance and went straight up to intensive care.

'I've come to see Mike Thomas,' she said to the nurse in the entrance.

'He's been moved. He's now in Ward Seven.'

'Oh. Is that good news?'

'Oh yes, indeed. He was brought round this morning and he immediately began shouting for attention. He's fine.'

'I see. Thank you very much.' She found Ward Seven and went in.

'Joanne,' came a voice from the side. 'Thanks so much for coming.' She crossed over to him and sat down.

'How are you feeling?' she asked politely. He looked terrible. A large bandage was wrapped round his head and he had bruises all over him. He also had a black eye to add to his discomfort.

'I'm fine. Well, a bit weak but I'm so pleased to see you. Mum said you were here last night when I was out of it. They patched me up and now I just want to go home.'

'Don't be in too much of a hurry. I was sorry to hear about Sarah.' She spoke carefully, unsure if he knew of her demise.

'Yes, that's so sad.'

'Why was she with you in the car?'

'I was taking her back to her home. It was her fault that I crashed. I say, have you heard anything about the car? Is it salvageable?'

'I've got no idea.'

'I bet Mel's in a stew over it.'

'He was okay last night when I spoke to him. He sends his best wishes to you, in case nobody's told you yet.'

'Thanks. You spoke to him?'

'I wanted to know if he knew why Sarah was in the car with you.'

'I told you. She had been pestering me stupid all weekend. I finally met her and decided to take her home. She was being so ridiculous. She leaned over me and I think she must have tugged on the steering wheel. I don't really remember what happened. I think I hit my head and was knocked out cold. That'll teach me won't it?'

'I suppose it will.'

'Joanne . . . please say you forgive me. Please, let's get back together again. It's been hell since . . . well, since we weren't really together.'

'You just concentrate on getting yourself well again. We'll see after you're recovered.'

'But that's going to take ages. I have this broken leg and all the other bits to get over. I need you to be beside me. Please Joanne.'

'I'll see. I'll come to see you till you're out of here. Will you go back to your home after that?'

'I guess so. Unless you'd like to take me in?'

'Don't be ridiculous. I'm a working woman. I can't possibly cope with you at my place.' Her words came out rather quicker than she'd intended.

'Yes, of course you are. Sorry for asking you. It was just me being hopeful. Come on then. Tell me the gossip from college. How's Trisha?'

'Fine as far as I know. I haven't seen her for a while actually. You know I went to see my parents at the weekend? No, of course you don't.' She realised that he couldn't have received her message. 'I went up on Friday evening. It was all very nice. I somehow missed your messages. Sorry.'

'And I there was me thinking you were deliberately cutting me out of your life.'

'I wouldn't do that,' she told him. 'I'm just not sure why you spent so much time with Sarah if you really disliked her so much.'

'I told you. She's a . . . she was a nutcase. She latched on to me about two years ago. She said to everyone that we were engaged and we never were. She really only came back on leave and thought she'd con a lot more money out of us. It was a tough time for her to be asking. That is it. I'm really sorry she'd dead. It's pretty tough for me to deal with. Her parents are also dead and I suppose she had problems with all of that. I'm sorry, but I can't let it spoil my life. Please Jo, let me know we can have a future. I never could quite allow myself to suggest it before — well, before Sarah was out of the way — but please, will you marry me?'

'I'll think about it. That's the best I can do at present. You've disrupted my life somewhat.'

'Think about it and let me know when you decide.'

'Of course I will. You've got to concentrate on healing yourself. Stop worrying about me and get better.'

Later that evening she sat at home and thought. She lay back on her sofa and thought long and hard. She assumed they'd live in her house. Would she want to share it with someone? It would be different. He would be there every evening. He would be there most of the time, interrupting her own plans and stopping her from working. It would be a forever thing. She wouldn't be free any more. Why couldn't they still see each other and, yes, maybe sleep together some of the time? She wanted him to sleep with her. He could return home whenever he wanted to. She had decided this was what she wanted, but somehow she didn't think he would accept it as a way of life. Only time would tell if it could work. What a mess, she thought.

Mike came out of hospital a week later. He'd decided to hand his notice in to the flat he shared with Mel and return home to live. Mel was delighted to get his place to himself and his girlfriend moved there to be with him. The car insurance would pay for a new car so with half each, Mel would not be stranded without some sort of vehicle. It was the end of another era. Mike's parents were pleased to get him home and his mother looked after him until he could move around more freely. Joanne was invited round for a Sunday lunch, one of the main things that always happened in their home.

'We thought we'd just leave it as the four of us rather than invite Sally and her brood. Hope this meets with everyone's approval?'

'Fine, thanks,' Joanne replied. 'Can I help you at all?'

'No, you're just fine. Talk to Mike before he drives us all mad with his demands. Talk about a bad patient.'

'Don't talk about me as if I'm not here,' he protested. 'Honestly, did you ever hear the like?'

'She loves you to bits,' Joanne told him. 'Give her leave to spoil you a bit.'

'A bit? She's spoiling me rotten. I don't have room to breathe. I'll try to behave for a bit longer, but don't expect me to stay here for too long. Please Jo, let me come to your place for a while? I promise not to be any trouble and I'll even cook for you. A pair of crutches and I'll manage fine.'

'Mike, please don't ask me to do that. I'm still thinking about your proposal. Honestly.'

'Now, who's for a drink?' asked his father, coming into the room and saving further conversation about marriage.

'A soft drink for me please. I'll have to drive home.'

'And a soft drink for you too, my boy. Can't have you mixing the potions now can we?' He poured each of them a glass of orange juice while he drank a small whisky. 'I'll take a sherry through to your mother.' He disappeared into the kitchen.

'All right, I accept that it will make a big change to your life marrying me. But think about it carefully, won't you? I can move in for a while for you to see how it will work.'

'Let's wait till you're better. You're still on heavy medication and it will be a while before you're clear of that. Relax and settle for being alive. I'm very pleased you are, by the way.'

'So am I. Very pleased.' He reached over and took her hand and pressed it to his lips. 'I'll be even more pleased when you say yes.'

She smiled at him, wondering how she could love someone so much and yet still couldn't commit herself to him so finally. She was much too selfish, she decided. The rest of the day was spent chatting to them all and no more questions about marriage were possible, much to her relief. She left early in the evening, saying she needed to get home to be prepared for the following day. Mike's parents left them alone for a few minutes to say goodbye.

'Please, do think carefully won't you?' he said.

'I've told you I will. Don't bank on it too much though, please. I do love you, you know that. Now I'm going home. Get better. I'll see you again very soon.'

'It won't be too soon for me. I love you, Joanne.'

She left them, knowing it wouldn't be long before she had to make her decision.

16

Joanne settled back into her usual routine, working hard and going out with the rest of the college crowd occasionally. It suited her. She went over to see Mike and his family at weekends and was pleased to see he was improving each time she saw him. He was extremely restless and wanted everything to happen immediately. The factory was managing to keep going and he was going in with his father a few times each week. He had even stopped asking her to marry him, which came as a great relief to her. She was very surprised when, one day when she was arriving, his mother asked her a question.

'I wondered if you could do us a huge favour?'

'If I can,' she replied.

'Could you possibly have Mike to

stay with you for a few days? He's fairly easily manageable now. He can move around really well and manage for himself but I don't like to leave him alone, here. I did ask Sally but it's difficult for them, with the children and all.'

'I suppose he could come and stay with me,' she replied carefully. 'What's happening?'

'Well, we want to go and look at a house and thought we'd take a couple of days away at the same time.'

'Oh, I see. Okay, if Mike's willing to come.'

'We know he's stayed with you before so he knows your house. It would be from Wednesday over the next weekend. We haven't told him about the plans yet, but if you're willing we'll do so right away.'

'Okay. That will give me some time to get ready for him. He'll be on his own for the days but I'll be back in time to do supper.'

'Thanks so much. It means a lot to us to be able to go away for a day or two on our own.'

'That's fine.' She thought about it. Her decision time must be getting nearer.

'Hallo you two. I was wondering what you were gossiping about out there. Come and give me a kiss.' She did so and his mother watched them fondly.

'We were talking about you going to stay with Joanne for a day or two.' He looked at her questioningly.

'Your parents want to go away for a day or two and have asked if you can come to me. I did say yes, you'll be pleased to hear.'

'Oh wow. That's terrific. When exactly?'

'On Wednesday. We're going down to the coast until the weekend.'

'I see. Why so suddenly?'

'Just a short break,' she said, looking at Joanne with a warning not to say anything more.

'This must be a first. Are we closing the factory or am I expected to run that?'

'Your father is willing to shut down for a couple of days. He doesn't have much on the go at present and this seemed like a good chance.'

'Tell me about it. There hasn't been much on the go for weeks,' he said miserably. 'Where is he anyway?'

'He popped out for a bit. Won't be long. Now I'll go and see to lunch.'

'You're sure you're okay with this plan?' Mike asked her.

'I'm fine with it. You'll have to manage on your own for the day but I'll get back as soon as I can to fix dinner and so on.'

'Mum's such a fusspot. I'd be okay on my own here but being with you will be so much better.'

'Yes, well, it's a no-nonsense time. I shall put you in the spare room.'

'You really know how to spoil things don't you?' he teased. 'Here's me, near perfect in life and limb, and you're putting me in the spare room?'

'It's how *near* you really are that bothers me. We'll see anyway.'

'I do love a bossy woman.' He paused. 'Is it because I'm too young for you?'

'What?'

'Is this why you won't give me an answer?'

'Of course not. It's just that, well, I'm not certain I even want to be married. If I did, you'd be my first choice, I am sure of that.' His face fell and he looked terribly miserable. 'Hey, cheer up. You're coming to stay for a few days. I'll have to fetch you on Tuesday evening. Only the day after tomorrow.'

'Yes, maybe you're right. I'll cheer up instantly.' He tried so hard but each time she looked him, she caught a glimpse of his sad face.

Joanne drove to his parents' house after work on Tuesday evening. His mother had prepared dinner for them.

'I thought it would save you the bother, dear,' she told her.

'That was nice of you. We still have plenty of time to get him settled. Are you all packed and ready to go in the morning?' Joanne asked her.

'I think so. Mind you, getting my husband to settle what he wants to take is quite a chore.'

'Getting Dad to do anything is difficult. You are all okay with this?' he asked Joanne.

'Course I am. Looking forward to having you to stay.' She really meant it, she realised. It was going to be lovely to have him in her house, staying for a few days ... even if they didn't sleep together.

When they reached her home he walked into the house using his crutches and smiled.

'It's so good to be here again,' he told her. 'Come here.' He enveloped her in his arms and kissed her and then fell onto the sofa, dragging her down with him.

'Watch it, my hero. You nearly broke my legs as well. You need to be careful.'

'I've worked out exactly how we can do it.'

'Do what?'

'What do you think? It means you taking charge and lying on top of me. I've got it all planned. Haven't had much else to think about lately.'

'We'll see. I'll take your bag upstairs now and leave it in the spare room.'

'It won't be needed in there. I intend to sleep with you. For the rest of this week and for as long as you'll allow me to.'

'Why do you think your parents wanted to go and look at a new house?' she asked him some while later.

'What?'

'They wanted to go and look at another house. Then to stay in the area for a while. I wondered if they said anything to you?'

'Nothing at all. I wonder if this means . . . do you think Dad could be about to retire?'

'I've no idea. Is it likely? I mean to say, he isn't that old is he?'

'Not quite. Interesting though. I say, if he isn't going to sell the business, maybe he's going to let us run it. Me and Sally, I mean.' His excitement was rekindled and he was busily talking it though for the rest of the evening.

'Look, you shouldn't get too excited about it. You still have some recovering to do. I may be quite wrong anyway. Suppose the house they want to look at isn't for them at all?'

'I can't think who else it might be. Anyway, let's forget about them for a bit. Concentrate on us. Isn't it bedtime yet?'

'It's not yet nine o'clock.'

'Wow, then we need to go to bed. It takes me an age to get upstairs. It's okay. I can manage by myself, given the time.' She watched as he made his way up the stairs. He had evolved a way of doing it and was soon there. 'Now you weren't serious about me going into your spare room, were you?'

'I'd thought you might prefer to have a bed to yourself.'

'No way. If I've got to sleep by myself, I'll go back to the hospital and demand a bed there.'

'Okay. If that's what you want.' She

was already feeling in need of him and wanting him very much. 'Shall I help you to undress?'

'Yes please.' He stood there and let her undress him.

'Have you got pyjamas in your bag?'

'No. I never put any in.'

'I see. Well, you'd better go to the bathroom first. Clean teeth and wash your face?' He hobbled along while she undressed. She pulled on her nightie and followed him to the bathroom. 'Managing all right?'

'Fine, thanks. Just about done. I hope you're not planning to wear that thing into bed?' he asked, tugging at her nightie. She laughed.

'Not at all. I'll be with you in a mo.' She looked at herself as she brushed her teeth. Let them see how the next few days went and she would give him her decision then.

She went along to the bedroom and peeled off her nightie.

'You must tell me what to do and when to stop,' she said.

'If I lie back here, you can make love to me all night if you have the energy.' He lay back and was waiting for her. She lay beside him and began to tease him.

When his parents returned home at the weekend, they phoned to ask how he was.

'So what have you two been doing?' he asked them.

'We wondered if we might come over to collect you?' his mother asked.

'Come over by all means. But I'm very happily ensconced here for a while longer.'

They arrived a while later and came inside.

'You look quite well, actually,' his mother told him.

'Good nursing. Mind you, it's largely self-nursing. She isn't the best of people to do that.' Jo slapped him on the shoulder. 'See what I mean?'

'Would you like some coffee? Or something to eat?' she invited.

'We need to talk to you both about

the future,' Mr Thomas told them.

'Fire away then,' Mike told him.

'We've put an offer in for a house. It's a smaller one than our place and very much less money.'

'And the factory?' Mike was interested to hear his plans.

'We thought you and Sally could take that on. You keep saying what you want to be done with it. Well, this is your chance. I took out a policy many years ago and it's now matured. Enough for us to live on, at least. I can always do something with my time.'

'Does Sally know about all of this?'

'Not yet. But I know how you two have been going on about it.'

'That's terrific, Dad. Thanks so much.'

'The only other thing is, where will you live?'

'I think I can stay here, for a while at least. Is that okay with you, Jo?'

'Of course.' At least this would give her some space to make sure they were going to work together. She had to

312

admit, it had been lovely for the last few days to know he would be there waiting for her. He'd even cooked dinner for them both on two occasions.

'Are you going to come back with us now?' his mother asked.

'Jo?'

'You can stay on if you want to. For as long as you want to,' she added, knowing it was the truth. She knew she would agree to them getting married. After all, she had once told her friends she was practically engaged to him, hadn't she?

THE END

HER HEART'S DESIRE
FROM THIS DAY ON
WHERE THE HEART IS
OUT OF THE BLUE
TOMORROW'S DREAMS
DARE TO LOVE
WHERE LOVE BELONGS
TO LOVE AGAIN
DESTINY CALLING
THE SURGEON'S MISTAKE

We do hope that you have enjoyed reading this large print book.

Did you know that all of our titles are available for purchase?

We publish a wide range of high quality large print books including:
Romances, Mysteries, Classics
General Fiction
Non Fiction and Westerns

Special interest titles available in large print are:
The Little Oxford Dictionary
Music Book, Song Book
Hymn Book, Service Book

Also available from us courtesy of Oxford University Press:
Young Readers' Dictionary
(large print edition)
Young Readers' Thesaurus
(large print edition)

For further information or a free brochure, please contact us at:
Ulverscroft Large Print Books Ltd.,
The Green, Bradgate Road, Anstey,
Leicester, LE7 7FU, England.
Tel: (00 44) **0116 236 4325**
Fax: (00 44) **0116 234 0205**

Other titles in the
Linford Romance Library:

GIRL WITH A GOLD WING

Jill Barry

It's the 1960s, and Cora Murray dreams of taking to the skies — so when her father shows her a recruitment advertisement for air hostesses, she jumps at the chance to apply. Passing the interview with flying colours, she throws herself into her training, where she is quite literally swept off her feet by First Officer Ross Anderson. But whilst Ross is charming and flirtatious, he's also engaged — and Cora's former boyfriend Dave is intent on regaining her affections . . .

THE SURGEON'S MISTAKE

Chrissie Loveday

Matti Harper has been in love with Ian Faulkner since their school days. He is now an eminent cardiac surgeon, she his theatre nurse. Ian has finally fallen in love — the trouble is, it's with Matti's flatmate Lori! But whilst a heartbroken Matti prepares to be their bridesmaid, Lori is being suspiciously flirtatious with another man. How can Matti tell Ian without appearing to be jealous? Best man Sam Grayling tries to help, but only succeeds in sending things from bad to worse . . .

DANCE OF DANGER

Evelyn Orange

Injured ballet dancer Sonia returns to her family home, Alderburn Hall, to discover that her cousin Juliette is dead. Clues point to Lewis, Juliette's widower, being responsible — yet Sonia still finds herself falling in love with him ... Several mysterious 'accidents' threaten not only her, but also Lewis's small daughter. Is Sonia in true danger? Can she discover the culprit? And can she and Lewis ever count on a future together?

THE UNFORGIVING HEART

Susan Udy

When wealthy businessman Luke Rivers asks Alex Harvey to utilise her specialist skills and decorate parts of his newly purchased home, she is determined to refuse. For this is the man who was responsible for practically destroying her family, something she can never forgive — or forget. Events, however, conspire against her in the shape of her demanding and increasingly rebellious younger brother Ricky and, despite her every instinct warning against it, she finds herself doing exactly what Luke Rivers wants . . .

AUGUSTA'S CHARM

Valerie Holmes

Attending her stepfather's dinner, Augusta is surprised to find that all the guests are single men. She quickly realises that she is being offered to the highest bidder. Faced with few options, Augusta finds herself leaving her home with Mr Benjamin Rufus Blood, destined for a life in Australia. However, there is far more adventure to be encountered en route. With her maid by her side, Augusta has to rely on more than just her charm to face the unknown future.

A FEAST OF SONGS

Patricia Keyson

In an act of kindness, Ellie offers to look after her friend's great aunt Phyllis after she suffers a fall. She travels to East Anglia and is entranced by the seaside town of Fairsands as well as the handsome and charming shopkeeper and restaurateur, Joe. Instead of the relaxing time she was hoping for, though, Ellie finds herself the target of acts of sabotage. Thinking revenge is the motive, she suspects Joe's former girlfriend Amber. But is she really a *former* girlfriend . . . ?